"I'm not myself today,"

Molly said, walking away from Ben.

Ben was beside her in an instant. "Yourself doesn't kiss?" he teased.

"No," she answered forcefully.

"I'd like to amend that."

How could she even begin to be attracted to the man? she silently reprimanded herself. Let alone be swept off her feet. And with just one kiss!

It was crazy.

It would go away.

It had to go away. She didn't want any part of a romance or an emotional involvement or—or anything, with any man.

"I want to see you again," he said.

Her head sounded alarms.

But her heart did a somersault.

Dear Reader:

Romance readers have been enthusiastic about the Silhouette Special Editions for years. And that's not by accident: Special Editions were the first of their kind and continue to feature realistic stories with heightened romantic tension.

The longer stories, sophisticated style, greater sensual detail and variety that made Special Editions popular are the same elements that will make you want to read book after book.

We hope that you enjoy this Special Edition today, and will enjoy many more.

Please write to us:

Jane Nicholls
Silhouette Books
PO Box 236
Thornton Road
Croydon
Surrey
CR9 3RU

VICTORIA PADE
Shelter from the Storm

Silhouette Special Edition

Originally Published by Silhouette Books
a division of
Harlequin Enterprises Ltd.

First published in Great Britain in 1989 by Silhouette Books, Eton House, 18-24 Paradise Road, Richmond, Surrey TW9 1SR

© Victoria Pade 1989

Silhouette, Silhouette Special Edition and Colophon are Trade Marks of Harlequin Enterprises B.V.

ISBN 0 373 57680 3

23—8909

Made and printed in Great Britain

VICTORIA PADE

is the mother of two energetic daughters, Cori and Erin. She laments that she has never traveled beyond Disneyland and instead has spent time plugging away at her computer. She takes breaks from her writing by indulging in her favorite hobby—eating chocolate.

Other Silhouette Books by Victoria Pade

Silhouette Special Edition

Breaking Every Rule
Divine Decadence
Shades and Shadows

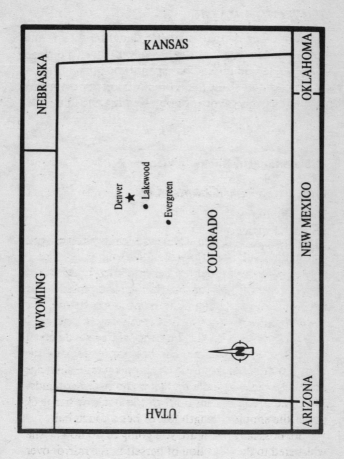

Chapter One

It was not a good sign when on Monday morning at eleven the week already seemed too long.

Molly Mercer sat behind her gray metal desk in the office of Mercer Moving and Storage and glared at the telephone she had hung up only moments before. She was in trouble, and it was just beginning to sink in.

With her hands on the desk top, she pushed herself to her feet and went into the bathroom, locking the door. Standing in front of the chipped white sink, she turned on the cold water and let it run over her hands. Then she pressed them both to the back of her neck under the shoulder-length fall of her auburn hair.

"So, boss lady, what are you going to do now?" she whispered to the reflection of herself in the mirror over the sink, not noticing that her pale skin was ashen, or that her green eyes were unnaturally wide beneath eyebrows that arched in bewilderment.

She didn't have an answer. But then she didn't have many answers these days. Lots of problems. Few solutions.

Mercer Moving and Storage had been a thriving business when she had come to work here right after college ten years before. Her grandfather had been anxious to delegate half of the responsibility to her, eager for semiretirement. But he had only been able to enjoy it for three years before her grandmother's cancer was discovered. In the five years that followed, the family and the family business had been financially depleted by medical bills. At the time of her grandmother's death a year ago, Mercer Moving and Storage was down to a measly four trucks and a single warehouse.

And now this.

Molly sighed and closed her eyes. They burned as if she hadn't blinked in hours.

Only six months had elapsed between the deaths of the grandparents who had raised her. Six months during which her grandfather had been distracted, preoccupied, grief-stricken. Six months during which she had taken on increasing business responsibilities, increasing work. But not all of it. And one of the few things that had been left to Ned Mercer was the renewal of the insurance coverage for anything stored in the warehouse.

Molly plunged her hands into the pockets of her khaki slacks and leaned forward, pressing the top of her head against the cool mirror.

The trucks were old and in need of repair, or better yet, of replacement. Bigger firms were luring drivers with better pay, more benefits. Competition was tough. And now a late summer rainstorm had seeped through the aluminum warehouse roof and damaged the antique furniture stored there. Furniture that should have been insured and wasn't.

"Molly? Are you in there?" Her secretary knocked on the door. "Did you want me to get the Petrys on the phone now?"

"No!" Molly's answer came swiftly as she jerked upright. She took a breath, breathed it out slowly and opened the door.

Taller than Molly's five-feet-two inches and heavier by at least forty pounds, Nancy Miller was a big woman. Her blond hair was streaked with a more platinum shade, and at that moment, her blue eyes were narrowed with concern. She stepped back and let her boss pass. "You look awful. What's happened now?"

Molly nodded toward the door that opened to the back of Nancy's desk and the rest of the warehouse beyond. "Close that and sit down, will you?" she asked of the woman who was also her friend.

Nancy did and then turned back to find Molly watering the philodendron on the windowsill with her morning cup of tea. "What's the matter?" Nancy reiterated.

Molly laughed a little. "You won't believe it when I tell you." She took another deep breath and finished in an ironic tone that hid her real concern. "We weren't covered."

Nancy's eyes widened. "The insurance? How can that be? Oh, no, Molly, don't tell me. I know your grandfather overlooked a lot of things at the end, but I gave him several warning notices that came from the insurance company, and I kept reminding him. I was sure when the warnings stopped that he had paid it."

"It wasn't your fault, Nancy."

"Are you sure there wasn't a mistake? Maybe the insurance company screwed things up."

Molly shook her head as she walked to stand behind the desk and flipped open the checkbook there. "Nope. I was on hold long enough to go back through the check registry. The last time he paid the premium was just before my grandmother died. It was due again eight months ago, and it was not paid."

"What does this mean?" Nancy asked hesitantly.

"It means we pay," Molly answered as if it were only a minor setback.

Nancy didn't look convinced that her boss was taking this lightly. Everyone who worked at Mercer Moving and Storage knew the business was floundering. Nancy knew more than most. "How will you make restitution?"

Molly shrugged. "I'll see if I can get the owners to accept payments. Then I just won't pull a paycheck for a while."

"I do payroll, remember? You haven't pulled a real paycheck in three months. You're taking a bare minimum for groceries and utilities at home and that's it."

Molly fiddled with some papers on her desk. "I'll work something out."

Nancy's voice was soft. "Maybe it's time you call it quits, Mol."

There wasn't a moment's hesitation before Molly shook her head vehemently. "No way. This company was my grandfather's baby. It's the family business. It's—"

Nancy cut her off. "It's not making it anymore."

"It's just in a hard time," Molly amended stubbornly. "All businesses go through slumps. We'll come out of it."

"I know what this means to you, but loyalty to your grandfather and sentimentality aren't going to keep you afloat."

"It isn't loyalty and sentimentality. Well, not entirely. It's my business—mine and my sister's—and I just won't let it go under." *You'll never understand it, Nancy, but I just can't let it go under. It's my grip on things.*

Her secretary looked dubious. "You could sell, you know. You'd come out with a little money—"

This time it was Molly who cut her off. "A little money—and when that's gone I'll have nothing. No future."

"You could invest it, go to work someplace where you didn't have all the burden, all the worry, all the responsibility. Wouldn't it be nice to have someone else handling all the hassles while you just cash your paycheck and make a regular life for yourself?"

Molly laughed. This was the lead-in to Nancy's weekly lecture. "A regular life being marriage. I don't want to get married, Nancy," she cut her friend off at the pass.

"You did once."

"I was young and dumb."

"Twenty is young, but thirty-three is hardly old."

"But I am smarter."

"Seriously, Molly. I'm worried about you. Sometimes you just have to know when to bail out."

Molly pushed up the sleeves of her red V-necked T-shirt. "I agree. But now is not the time."

The telephone rang, and Molly reached for it. "I'll answer this. See how fast you can get someone in here to assess the cost of replacement, and someone else who refinishes antiques to tell us what can be fixed instead of replaced. We weren't set to deliver that stuff for another two weeks. I'd rather not notify the Petrys until I have to and then I want to go armed with all the information I need."

"I know—full steam ahead. I'll do what I can," Nancy said as she left.

Molly picked up the phone. "Mercer Moving and Storage."

A sob answered her.

"Hello?"

"Molly?"

Adrenaline flooded her veins at the sound of her younger sister's voice. "Karen? What's wrong? Has something happened to one of the kids?"

"No," her sister barely managed to answer, and offered no more.

"Is it Carl? He's had an accident," Molly guessed, feeling cold and clammy all of a sudden.

Karen Dune broke into a fresh sob, but said nothing.

"Oh, my God, it is Carl. What happened?" Molly demanded urgently.

"The bastard," her sister nearly shouted on the other end.

Molly sat down in her chair, took a deep breath and asked in a calming tone, "Karen, will you tell me what's going on?"

"Can the kids and I come stay with you?"

"It's as much your house as it is mine. You know that. Please tell me what happened." Molly dropped her head forward and rubbed the back of her neck.

"An affair," Karen choked out in a tone garbled with tears. "He had an affair."

Molly stopped massaging the back of her neck. She straightened up. For a moment she didn't say anything. Instant rage erupted inside her. She tried to control it before she spoke and then realized she didn't know what to say. "I think I'd better come over there."

"No." Karen hiccupped. "We've talked it over and agreed that the girls and I need some time out. I'm going to throw a few things in a suitcase and go. He went for a walk, and I don't want to be here when he gets back. It makes it seem too . . . serious." She broke into fresh sobs on that last word.

A million questions ran through Molly's mind. She settled on one that answered nothing. "Are you all right to drive?"

Another hiccup. "It's only two miles."

"How are the kids? Do they know?"

That renewed the sobs. "They're rotten, of course. I sent them to their rooms, but they overheard the fight we had when it all came out. They know everything I do."

"God." Vivid memories upset her stomach. She forced herself not to think about it, to think about practical things—water damage and insurance—she could handle that. "Shall I meet you at the house?"

"I don't know. I can't think. One minute I want to be alone, and the next I'm crawling in my own skin and I need someone to distract me. I can't believe this is happening. I can't believe he did it. I can't talk anymore . . ."

"Karen," Molly said firmly to keep her from hanging up, "listen to me. I want you to call me when you get to the house. I'll come home and we'll go from there. You're not alone in this, you know."

"I know. I have to go throw up."

Her sister sounded pitiful, and it wrenched Molly's heart. "Are you going to be okay?"

Karen laughed hysterically. "Sure."

"You won't forget to call me, will you?"

"No. I'm really going to throw up, Molly."

The phone went dead on the other end.

Molly replaced the receiver but didn't let go of it. It seemed as though there should be something she could do, someone she could call for help. But there wasn't. She was it.

She dragged her hand away and fell back in her desk chair.

Carl Dune, you bastard.

Don't think about it. Think about water damage and insurance.

Good grief, what else could happen today?

The office door opened slightly, and Nancy stuck her head in. "There's a man here to see you."

Molly stared at her friend for a moment before the announcement sank in. "Did I forget an appointment?"

"No. His name is Ben Boyd, and he says he has to speak to you on a personal matter."

"I don't know anyone named Ben Boyd. Get rid of him for me, Nancy. That was Karen on the phone, and there's trouble in paradise. My quota for surprises today is filled."

"I'll try," the secretary answered dubiously. "But you might be making a mistake. He's some kind of hunk."

Molly shook her head, made a little sound of frustration and ducked for cover behind her own hands. "Don't you ever think about anything else? I don't care if he looks like Cary Grant, just get rid of him."

Nancy laughed at her and closed the door.

When it opened again a few minutes later, it was not the secretary whose face poked through the crack. It was, indeed, some kind of hunk.

Molly looked up from her worries to see tanned skin and waves of sun-streaked hair the color of winter wheat. His eyes were silver-gray beneath eyebrows that were just slightly bushy and unruly. His face was rawboned and angular, his nose thin, his jaw square and sharp, his cheekbones pronounced above deep hollows.

His expression was very somber. "Are you Molly Mercer?" he asked in a voice that was low and resounding.

Molly swallowed and remembered she was not a teenager beholding incredible male beauty for the first time. Her tone was frosty. "I'm sorry, but I can't possibly see you today. If you'll leave your card, or a name and number, I'll try to get in touch with you when I can."

"If you're Molly Mercer, this can't wait."

Molly sighed, arched an eyebrow his way and put an even sharper edge into her tone of voice. "I'm sure whatever you're selling is very important to you, but I am in the middle of chaos here. I assure you there will be a better time."

"I'm not selling anything. There's something I have to tell you. Today."

He looked grimly determined. What now?

Molly glanced at the round clock on the wall beside the door and said like a drill sergeant, "I'll give you five minutes, and this had better be good."

"It isn't good at all," he said seriously as he stepped into her office and closed the door behind him.

Dressed in khaki slacks and a button-down shirt with the long sleeves rolled midway between thick wrists and elbows, he was very tall, very broad, very muscular, very powerful looking and very attractive. He seemed to fill her office in a way that took command of the space. Oddly, it unnerved Molly more than anything else that had happened that day.

She sat up straighter and motioned him to a chair, feeling as if the reins of control were in his large, strong-looking hands. She resented that, and at the same time was oddly enlivened by it.

Everything was off kilter today. Maybe she was really at home, in bed, asleep, and this was all a nightmare.

But he smelled faintly of a pine forest after a spring rain, a scent that was almost intoxicating, and Molly knew he was real. Probably real trouble. And she didn't need any more of that right now.

"You are Molly Mercer, aren't you?" he asked again in that rich baritone.

What was he, a summons server? she wondered. That's all she needed now—someone was probably suing her. She sighed impatiently. "Yes, I am Molly Mercer."

"Daughter of John Northrup?"

Trouble came in threes, she thought at the mention of that name. "Yes," she answered icily.

The man took a deep breath and looked away from her. "I don't quite know how to say this," he admitted. "My name is Ben Boyd. I own Boyd's restaurants. I met your father after college. I worked for him in California, got to be friends with him, eventually became his business partner."

Molly stared at the man, confused, leery and feeling a sense of dread. But she said nothing. She didn't know what to say.

Ben Boyd shook his head as if he wasn't pleased with how he was handling whatever it was he'd come to say. His steely gaze came back to her, those semi-bushy brows in a perplexed frown. "I'm sorry. I know I'm confusing you. I'm pretty confused myself. I was friends with John for the past twelve...no, thirteen, years, and up until a month ago I didn't know he had ever been married or had kids..." He leaned forward in his chair and pierced her with his eyes. "If there's an easy way to say this, I don't know what it is." He sighed and finished very gently, "Your father died yesterday."

Molly was stone still.

"I'm sorry," he repeated compassionately.

She could feel her heart beat. She could hear it drum in her ears.

She was nine years old, and her father was grinning down at her in that mischievous, boyish way he had, holding his hand out to her and saying, "Let's go exploring..."

The surface of her skin prickled.

"*I love you, baby,*" she heard him say in her mind as vividly as if he were in the room with her.

Her eyes filled and stung.

"Are you all right? Can I get you something?" It was Ben Boyd's deep baritone voice bringing her back to the present. To reality.

Molly blinked back the tears before they could fall. She stood abruptly and swung to peer out of the small window that faced the parking lot, her arms hugging her middle.

Count the tires on the trucks. Two in front, four in the middle, eight in back. Would it rain more today? Have Nancy call for a weather report. Move the antiques to the other side of the warehouse. Get a roofer over here today. Karen . . . oh, God.

"Molly?"

Ben Boyd used her name as if they were close friends. How could there be such warmth in his voice? Maybe it just seemed so because she was so cold.

"Molly? Take a drink of this."

He was standing right beside her, towering over her, holding out the mug with what was left of her second cup of tea in it. Inexplicably, the close proximity of his big, powerful body and the thoughtfulness in the gesture made her feel safe. Maybe she was going crazy.

She took the mug because it seemed easier than refusing, but she didn't drink. Instead she cleared her throat. "How did he die?" she managed, surprising herself with the strength in her own voice.

"He had cancer," Ben Boyd informed her softly.

"My grandmother had cancer," she answered inanely, like a child who doesn't know what else to say.

She felt him reach out to her, begin to put his arm around her and then stop. Instead he took her elbow in a firm grip.

"Come and sit down."

But Molly didn't move from the window. She stayed staring out at the lot. Mercer Moving and Storage, it said on the sides of the trucks. Ned Mercer's company. She wasn't nine years old. So many years had passed. So many things had happened. Her father had gone on exploring without her....

Molly laughed a little then, and glanced up at Ben Boyd. He looked so worried. *Nice man.* The thought came on its own. *Get a hold of yourself, Molly.*

"I'm okay," she said, gaining control of her thoughts. "And I'm sorry I was nasty to you before. It's bad enough to come on a grim errand without getting a leper's reception in the process. Were you very close to my father?" she finished, sounding formal, aloof.

Ben Boyd looked at her strangely, as if he didn't quite understand what had happened. "Pretty close, yes. Like I said, we were friends for a long time, *partners...*"

Molly smiled consolingly up at him. "Then his death must have upset you. I'm sorry you had to come here and be the one to tell me. Would you like a cup of coffee or tea?"

Now he looked at her as if she were out of her mind. "No, thank you. Is there somebody I could call to be with *you*?"

"Oh, that's not necessary. I'm just fine. A little embarrassed at how I treated you, but fine." She moved away from the window, freeing herself from his grip on her elbow, to set the mug down on her desk. "This has not been one of my better days." Molly gave a rueful little laugh at the understatement.

"There was another reason I came today," he said as he went back around to the front of her desk, watching her intently as he did.

"Sit down, please," Molly said as she did likewise, all business now. She pretended not to notice the mixture of confusion and concern in his expression.

He hesitated uncertainly before saying, "Your father asked me to make the funeral arrangements. If you'd like to come with me, that would be fine. If not, I'll need to know if there's anything special you or your sister want in the service."

How could her palms be sweaty when she still felt so cold? "My sister is in the middle of a personal crisis, but I assure you neither she nor I have any preference. Whatever you decide will be fine. I..." She cleared her throat again. Why did it keep clogging like this? "I'm afraid I don't have any idea where he's been living. Where will he be buried?" she finished impersonally.

Ben Boyd's eyebrows arched in what looked like surprise. "He said you had drifted apart, but I assumed you at least knew... He's lived in California for the past twenty-one years. But he wanted to be buried here."

"I see. When do you plan to have the service?"

"When do *I* plan to have..." He looked astounded and then as if realization had dawned, he said, "I know, this has been a shock. Of course it has to be soon, within the next few days. What would you prefer?"

Molly's mouth was bone dry. She took a sip of the tepid tea in the mug. "You mean, what day would be best if I was going to attend it?"

"I didn't think there was any question that you would attend it."

She took another drink of tea. Why wasn't her brain functioning? "Of course," she agreed indecisively. "The day doesn't matter. Just let me know what you've arranged."

Just then Nancy poked her head in the door again. "Excuse me, Molly, but I thought you'd want to know I've found one man who can assess the value of the antiques and give you an estimate on refinishing. Should I set something up with him?"

Business. Molly seized it like a lifeline. "Yes, please. But check with Bruce to see if he can deal with him. Karen needs me at home as soon as I'm finished here."

When Nancy had retreated, Molly looked back at Ben Boyd, finding him studying her. She gave him her best this-meeting-is-over smile. "Is there anything else?"

He paused. "There is, but this isn't the time to discuss it. If you give me a number where you can be reached, I'll call as soon as I've made the arrangements and fill you in on the details."

Molly took one of her business cards from her desk drawer and wrote her home phone number on the back of it. As she handed it to him, she said, "I appreciate your coming here to tell me. And again, I apologize for making it hard for you to get in." It was an obvious dismissal.

He stood and went to the door, but before leaving he turned a beetled brow back to her. "You're sure you'll be all right?"

"Positive, thank you."

He didn't look convinced, but he opened the door anyway. "I'm sorry," he said, as if he was reluctant to leave her and couldn't think of anything else to say.

This time when Molly smiled, her cheeks quivered. "Yes, well..." Once more she cleared her throat. "Thanks."

He hesitated another moment, but in the end left her alone in her office.

Molly continued to stare at the door long after it was closed, but it wasn't the present she was seeing.

First she was nine and tagging along with her father as he played tennis, trying to hit the ball just the way he'd shown her.

That image made her throat clog, her eyes mist.

Then she was twelve. Her security was shattered. She was sick to her stomach. And so afraid.

She knew she shouldn't care a wit that John Northrup was dead, but she did.

Chapter Two

Ben's mind was not on his driving as he maneuvered his vintage black Jaguar east on Colorado's I-25 through the late-August drizzle. His thoughts weren't on the grim funeral duty he was on his way to performing. Instead he was mulling over a dozen questions about John Northrup's revelation a mere month before that he had once been married and had fathered two children.

Ben couldn't help thinking how strange it was that he had really known very little about a man he had considered his friend.

They had met in the seventies when Ben had moved to San Diego for a taste of living in the sunshine instead of the snow. He had just graduated from college with a business degree, but his heart hadn't been in corporate America, it had been in food—a lifetime passion—and so he had opted for learning the restaurant business. Answering an ad, he had been hired for a management trainee position in the French restaurant John Northrup owned.

A shared passion for tennis had begun their friendship. But then, John's relationship with all his employees had been less than formal. A likable man, John was confident, almost cocky, quick witted, funny and energetic to the point of hyperactivity. He had been a good businessman, if a bit erratic in his work habits, but beyond that, he hadn't taken anything too seriously. He had loved all sports and participated with an intense competitiveness in many, and he had a somewhat naive vision of the world. His personality had put him on more of a peer level with his young employees, in spite of the fact that he was thirty years older. At the time his youthful, carefree attitude had seemed admirable. He had been fun—one of the guys.

Ben pushed a U2 tape into the cassette deck, wondering for the first time if it was such a good thing for a fifty-five-year-old man to be one of the guys with twenty-two-year-olds. Thinking about himself, he realized that at thirty-five he already felt a world away from his own employees who were in their early twenties. And yet until his death at sixty-eight, John had had friends much, much younger than he.

The melancholy strains of The Joshua Tree filled the tan interior as Ben pondered his relationship with John Northrup. Ben had spent seven years in San Diego working with John. During that time they had become good friends. Up until recently, Ben would have said close friends. But now he knew better.

They had been good enough friends for John to offer backing for a restaurant of Ben's own when Ben had decided he missed not only his family in Colorado, but the snow he had wanted to get away from before. John had been a good enough friend to keep his forty-percent share of Ben's restaurants silent, to accept whatever decisions Ben made about the expansions that had multiplied Boyd's into two, and then, as of last month, three highly rated, profitable establishments. Good enough friends to confide his illness when he learned he had cancer. But not close enough friends to tell him about his two daughters until he was dying and legal details needed to be dealt with.

If he was honest with himself, Ben realized that he resented that.

He also couldn't help wondering why his friend had left everyone believing he had never been married.

A month ago John had asked Ben to come to San Diego. Once there, the older man had merely stated that he had two daughters from an early marriage and was leaving his forty percent of Boyd's restaurants to them. He and his daughters had drifted apart, John had said, and beyond the stipulations he wanted Ben to follow, he had gone into no more detail.

Stunned at first, and left without any explanations, Ben had assumed a number of things. He had assumed that John had been married very early in his life. He had pictured Molly Mercer and her younger sister well into their forties. His scenario had them hitting adulthood, probably in marriages of their own, about the time John had moved to San Diego more than twenty years before. John, he had further assumed, must surely have had some contact with his daughters, but probably hadn't talked about them because it had been painful for him not to have had a close relationship. This was a scenario Ben could accept.

Until he met Molly Mercer and none of those assumptions had fitted.

Molly Mercer couldn't be older than thirty-one or thirty-two. And she hadn't even known where her father lived.

Somehow estrangement seemed a better description than drifting apart.

And yet, a month ago when John had told him about his daughters, he hadn't seemed like an uncaring father. Removed, but not uncaring. In fact, Ben had assumed that it was concern for them that had inspired John to extract a specific promise from him over and above what was legally set out in the older man's will.

Now he wondered if it was a guilty conscience that had inspired it.

And here he had gone out today to find Molly Mercer to break the news that her father had died, to assure her that in consideration of the grief he assumed she and her sister would feel Ben would make the funeral arrangements.

So much for assumptions.

She had been upset—he could tell that. But she hadn't even been sure she would come to the funeral, let alone be one of the two principal mourners.

Ben eased off the highway and merged with city traffic en route to the mortuary.

"Did you even know what a beautiful daughter you had, John?" he asked of the air, a vivid picture of Molly Mercer in his mind's eye.

Her hair was a shade less than red. Auburn was what it was, a rich, cocoa-brown color with highlights like hot flames. Fiery beauty—that was his impression of her. She didn't look at all like her father, except maybe in the litheness of her body, in her long, thin arms and legs. If the sparkle in those green eyes was any indication, she might have his humor, and even if she didn't, the sparkle alone was incredibly attractive. Her face was fine boned, her skin smooth and creamy. Ben had had such an urge to run the backs of his fingers along her cheek to see if it really was as velvety as it appeared.

"She strikes me as remarkable, John. Did you know that?"

And there hadn't been a wedding ring in sight....

Ben felt a twinge of guilt. This was no time to find himself attracted to Molly Mercer. Standing at the window in her office, he had wanted to take her into his arms, to comfort her grief, but he had also wanted to hold her in a way that had nothing at all to do with consolation.

"What are you thinking about, Boyd?" he said wryly to himself. "You were her father's friend, for crying out loud. Her father just died. And here you are feeling lucky, as though you've met a one-in-a-million woman on a blind date. She's John's daughter." He drew the words out long and slow, as if it would have more effect that way.

But no matter how hard he tried, Ben couldn't think of John as a father. Fathers were mature, and that description didn't fit John. In fact, there had been times when Ben had felt more mature than his friend.

Still, that didn't change the fact, his conscience chided.

But as Ben pulled into the mortuary parking lot, attraction was winning the battle with his conscience.

Regardless of the circumstances, he couldn't get it out of his mind that Molly Mercer did seem like a one-in-a-million woman.

It wasn't until after four that Molly drove her conservative Toyota into the driveway of the old red-brick Victorian-style house that had been built by her grandparents early in their marriage. A two-story, steeply roofed structure, it sat far back on a half-acre lot that her grandfather had kept in immaculate condition. Thinking of him, Molly had followed his yearly practice of planting yellow and purple pansies in all the flower beds.

Her sister's white station wagon was parked on the street, and from it Molly's ten-year-old niece, Melissa, was carrying a box of stuffed animals.

"Hi, Lissa," Molly greeted as the grim-faced little girl drew near. "How are you?"

Melissa Dune shrugged and cast her eyes downward. "Okay, I guess."

Molly took the box of toys, balanced it on her right hip, and put her other arm around the girl's narrow shoulders. She leaned near to her ear and whispered, "Everything will be all right, kiddo."

Lissa nodded halfheartedly, obviously unconvinced, and said in an angry tone, "I just wish Beth would stop crying all the time."

Beth was her eight-year-old sister. "It's okay to cry when something awful happens, don't you think?" Molly suggested.

"Not all the time. She never stops," the little girl grumbled.

"How about your mom? How's she doing?" Molly asked as they climbed the four cement steps to the wide, covered porch.

The ten-year-old's eyes filled at the mention of her mother. "Not so good. She cries a lot, too."

Molly gave her a squeeze and then let go to open the carved front door. "Guess we better see what we can do about it, huh?"

Again the shrug, this time helplessly, but she said nothing as she preceded her aunt into the house.

It was quiet and cool inside. Molly set the box of stuffed animals on a deacon's bench in the entrance and turned right, through an archway, into the living room. The room was decorated in a cozy country style, and the walls had oak chair rails that bordered a navy blue wallpaper with tiny beige flowers. Cream colored tic-back curtains separated the picture window from the fanlight above it.

Her sister sat on the hearth of the manteled fireplace, sniffling into a Kleenex. Slightly taller than Molly, childbearing and being a good cook had put several extra pounds on Karen Dune. Molly knew that of the two of them, it was Karen who resembled their father, especially in her honey-blond hair and blue eyes. Ordinarily, Karen was an attractive woman. But with her hair pulled straight back into a ponytail and her face puffy and blotched from crying, she looked as miserable as she felt.

She glanced up as Molly and Melissa entered the room. "Well, hi," she said in a strained voice. "Did you get your critters, Lissa?"

"Yeah," the little girl mumbled, staring at the tan carpet rather than looking at her mother's angst-ridden face.

Molly smoothed a stray curl from her niece's eyes, cupped her chin to raise it and winked comfortingly down at her. "Why don't you go upstairs and see if you can make Beth smile while I talk to your mom?"

Lissa didn't need more prompting. She turned and fled as if she'd rather be anywhere in the world than in the room at that moment.

The two women watched her go, and then Molly turned back to her sister. "How about a cup of tea with a good stiff shot of brandy in it?"

Karen managed a sad laugh. "You and Grandpa. He always thought a hot toddy worked miracles, too. You know I hate tea."

"Then how about just the good stiff shot of brandy?"

Karen grimaced, and her lips paled to the same color as her skin. "I can't keep anything down."

"Come and sit with me, then. I could use a cup of tea."

Karen followed her sister through an archway off the living room into a large kitchen. A round pedestal table with four high-backed chairs dominated the center of the room, around which were oak cupboards, the most modern appliances and cheery white wallpaper sprigged with golden wheat. Tea was only an excuse to move into the kitchen. In all the years they had lived here, that room had been the one in which all crises had been faced.

Molly put water on to heat and sat beside her sister at the table, watching her. Karen fiddled nervously with a place mat, saying nothing.

"Do you want to talk about it?" Molly asked without pushing.

Karen shrugged much the same as Lissa had before. "I told you, Carl's been acting weird for the past few months."

"You thought it was the problems he was having at work."

"Guess I was wrong."

Tears streaked down Karen's cheeks again. Molly got her a fresh Kleenex from the box on top of the white refrigerator, trying hard to keep her own anger at her brother-in-law hidden. When she handed the tissue to her, Karen went on.

"He says it only happened once—three months ago. It was with his assistant. They were commiserating over drinks on that last business trip when he lost the advertising account for those new crackers. They'd had too much to drink, and one thing led to another...."

"So why the confession now?" Molly closed her eyes and sighed at the lack of control that had made her voice sound harsh and judgmental.

"I know what you're thinking," Karen shot back. "That he's lying. That no one has a one-night affair. That it's probably been going on for the whole three months."

"I didn't say that. Besides, it doesn't matter what I think. What matters is what you think."

The misery on her sister's face was answer enough. Rather than say what she thought, Karen blew her nose, breathed a ragged breath and finally answered Molly's question. "The assistant wanted more than a one-night stand and was threatening to call me herself. He says he thought he'd better be the one to tell me."

"What a guy." Molly's facetiousness only served to bring on a fresh flood of tears. She immediately regretted it. "I'm sorry."

Karen looked at her pointedly. "It isn't the same, you know."

Molly stood up abruptly to fix her tea. "Are you sure of that?"

Karen's hesitation said that she wasn't. "He wants to go on from here. He didn't want me to leave. He said he didn't have any intention of leaving me, that it was just a mistake he made once. It'll never happen again."

Molly dipped her tea bag over and over, not looking at her sister. "Just a mistake," she repeated. *Keep your mouth shut, Molly—it's her life*. She went back to the kitchen table with her steaming cup of tea and sat down again.

Karen squeezed her eyes shut and grimaced. "I feel like the top of my head is going to blow off."

Molly frowned. "Have you taken your blood-pressure medicine?"

Karen nodded without opening her eyes to her sister's concern. "Having the same hypertension that killed your mother when you're fourteen tends to make you very careful about taking the stuff to control it. I just don't think it's working today."

"You'd better call your doctor and see about getting a mild tranquilizer."

Karen dropped her head to her crossed arms on the tabletop, groaning as she did. "I can't face airing my dirty laundry in order to get them."

"I'll call," Molly insisted, frightened for her sister's safety.

"Good, I just can't," came Karen's muffled answer. Then she sat up and reached for Molly's teacup, taking a small sip. "I always thought I had such a great marriage, such a great guy in Carl, that I was so lucky. I was always sure that if only you could find someone just like him, you'd see for yourself that not all men are..." Karen gulped on a sob. "Now I'm beginning to think you were the lucky one to have Dave call off your wedding and spare you this."

Molly laughed wryly at that. "Shocked to have him announce two days before the ceremony that he just couldn't go through with that kind of commitment, embarrassed to have to call everybody we knew and tell them not to come, but in a way you're right—it was lucky it happened before the wedding rather than after."

"I'm sorry," Karen said quickly. "I shouldn't have said that. I know how it hurt you and deepened old wounds. I'm just not thinking straight."

"I wasn't taking offense," Molly assured her. "I'd better call your doctor before it gets any later."

She went to the phone beside the archway that connected the living room, but just as she reached for the receiver, the phone rang.

"If that's Carl, I don't want to talk to him," Karen instructed frantically.

"All right," Molly said in a calming tone, motioning for her to sit back in her chair. "I'll take care of it."

She answered in an I'm-ready-to-do-battle tone of voice, but it wasn't Carl Dune on the other end. It was Ben Boyd. Unreasonably, Molly felt a warm rush of pleasure at the sound of his rich baritone.

"How are you doing?" he asked immediately, his concern seeming genuine.

For a split second Molly had forgotten the news he had delivered that morning. When she remembered, she also remembered that she had been debating with herself all day whether to tell Karen. She still didn't have a resolution to the debate. "I'm fine, thanks."

"I wanted to let you know that I've made most of the arrangements. The service will be tomorrow morning at ten. Is that okay for you?"

"Tomorrow morning at ten," Molly repeated, mentally rearranging her schedule. "Sure, that's okay."

"There are a couple of things I need to know. This is the first time I've done something like this, and I didn't realize all it entailed. Are you up to some grim questions?"

"No, but I don't suppose I have a choice."

"I'm sorry. Here comes the worst one. I need to tell the mortuary if you want to view the body."

There was that clog in her throat again. Molly cleared it. "No."

"What about your sister? Do you know if she'll want to?"

Did she know if Karen wanted to? She couldn't imagine that Karen would want to see their father at any time, let alone now. And yet, her sister was an adult. John Northrup was her father, too.

"Are you still there, Molly?" Ben asked gently.

"Yes, I'm still here. I can't answer that right at the moment. I'll have to ask her and I haven't broken the news to her yet."

"Would you like me to?" he offered compassionately.

Nice man. For the second time today that thought came on its own. "No, it's something I have to do. I just haven't found the right moment. How soon do you need an answer?"

"Fairly soon. Maybe I should ask you the rest so you can discuss it all with your sister and then get back to me with the whole thing."

"Good idea," she answered vaguely, feeling Karen's curious gaze on her back by now.

"I need to know if you want a limousine for the family and a procession to the cemetery."

Strange. This had to be the strangest day of her life. She kept having the sensation of floating back and forth in time, in and out of rooms, as if one minute she was involved and in control, and the next she was outside, watching a lot of things happening that she was removed from and wondering why she was expected to have answers to all these questions.

"Are you sure you're all right?" Ben asked when the second silence had elapsed.

He must think she was crazy. Irrationally, she didn't want him to think she was crazy at all. "Give me a number where I can call you back and I'll let you know."

"You'll let me know if you're all right?" he sounded confused and more concerned than ever.

"No, I'm definitely all right. I mean I'll let you know about . . . what you've just asked me."

He gave her two phone numbers and then the addresses of both his apartment and the restaurant he'd be at for the next few hours. "If you want to talk or you want to get out, feel free to call me or just come by. Or if you want me to come to you, just let me know. This isn't an easy time. You shouldn't be alone.''

Too late. He already must have been thinking she was on the edge. "Thanks, but I'm not really an emotional wreck. It just seems that way because I have more things going on right now than you can possibly imagine. I'll get back to you within an hour so you can finish the arrangements.''

"Whatever you say." He didn't sound convinced. "But I meant what I said. Just call.''

Molly thanked him again, hung up and turned slowly to face her sister.

"What was all that about?" Karen asked the moment the receiver was back on the hook.

Molly took a deep breath and sat down at the table again. She suddenly had strong sympathy for Ben Boyd's difficulty in knowing how to break this news to her this morning. Much as he had, she began with an explanation. "That was a man named Ben Boyd. He came by the office today. He was a friend of Dad's.'' Another notch on the strange meter—Dad. The familiarity just didn't feel right. And yet, what else was she to call him?

"Dad?" Karen repeated, as if her sister had referred to someone by their first name when that same person had always been known more formally.

Not knowing what else to say, Molly got it all out in the open. "Ben Boyd came to tell us that he died yesterday.''

Molly watched as Karen suddenly became dry eyed. She looked stunned, shocked, dumbstruck. "I know,'' Molly went on, "I wasn't sure what I should feel, either.''

"I can't handle this right now," Karen whispered on the verge of an even greater flood of tears.

"Of course you can't. That's understandable. But I was afraid if I didn't tell you, you'd resent it. You don't have to do anything, Karen. You really don't. God knows, neither of us owes him anything. I just wanted to make sure you had the chance to do whatever you might need to to deal with it."

Karen's eyes were glazed. It scared Molly, and again she had the sensation that there should be someone else she could call for help. "Are you sure you don't want that shot of brandy?" she said feebly.

Karen shook her head. "How? Where?" she barely managed to ask.

Molly repeated what she had been told and then the reasons for Ben Boyd's phone call moments before. "I don't want to see him," Molly told Karen firmly. "I'll go to the service, but I don't want a family car or a procession or any big deal. If you do, I'll need to tell him, but I don't think you should feel obligated, particularly not now."

"I'm going to be sick again...." Karen ran for the bathroom down the hall.

While she was gone, Molly found the number of her sister's doctor and called for the tranquilizers. When Karen came back she didn't sit down. Instead she leaned weakly against the archway from the living room. "I have to try and sleep. Tell whatever-his-name-is that I don't want to see...the body, either, or have a family car or a procession or anything. God, when it rains, it pours."

"You sounded just like Mama," Molly said softly.

"Poor Mama."

"Go lie down. I'll take care of everything."

"Poor Molly, you always do, don't you? I'm sorry."

Molly shrugged her sister's sympathy away and said matter-of-factly, "Somebody's got to do it."

"Now *you* sound like Mama." Karen pushed wearily away from the wall and headed for the stairs that led to the upper level.

"Hang in there, kiddo," Molly called after her with a false brightness. "Everything'll be okay. It always is."

"Sure, sure," Karen grumbled. "One way or another."

Molly turned the burner under the teakettle on again. While she waited for the water to heat, she picked up the slip of paper that had Ben Boyd's phone numbers and addresses on it. Into her thoughts came a sharp picture of the man—tall, muscular, handsome. She felt oddly soothed by the image and had an urge to do just as he had suggested, to go to him.

How bizarre.

Of course she would never do something like that. Why had it even occurred to her?

But then there was no logic in the rest of this day, so why shouldn't she feel like a stranger was shelter from the storm? Making as little sense as everything else did today, it fitted right in.

She poured her tea and let her mind linger on the image of Ben Boyd for a while. At this point, she'd take refuge wherever she could get it. Besides, it was just a harmless mental picture. It wasn't as if she was actually going to do anything....

Molly opened the pantry for a cookie to go with her tea and found the cupboard close to empty. With three other people in the house, and two of them growing kids, it was a situation she knew had to be immediately rectified.

Coincidentally, the grocery store was only a couple of blocks down the street from the restaurant Ben Boyd had said he'd be at for the next few hours. She had seen the place before and read about it in the newspaper—it was highly rated for steak, lobster and crab legs—but she had never been there. Small world.

She needed to call him, she reminded herself.

Then again...

Rather than make a phone call to answer the last of his funeral arrangement questions, she'd be nearby, anyway. She could just stop in...

Shelter from the storm, the thought came again.

She breathed a wry laugh at that. No man was shelter from the storm. Men *were* the storm.

Again she picked up the slip of paper, only this time she dialed one of the numbers on it. The line was busy. Molly hung up and tried again. Maybe she had dialed wrong. But again it was busy. Then she checked the clock on the stove. She had promised to get back to Ben Boyd in an hour. That had been forty-five minutes ago. She could drive there in ten. But if the phone line stayed busy another fifteen minutes, that would probably ruin the timetable Ben needed to keep to get her answers back to the mortuary for the funeral tomorrow morning.

And she needed groceries, anyway...

Molly dialed the number one last time, just in case. But once more she got a busy signal.

She had to let him know about the funeral arrangements. So what if in the meantime she managed to get a little solace for herself? It wasn't such a bad thing.

Everybody needed a little shelter from the storm now
and then....

Even if it was an illusion.

Boyd's Restaurant was just off Union Street in the
center of a hotel and office complex in Lakewood. It
was an elegant white building beside a pond that
dipped down amid lush green lawns. Two snow-white
ducks floated on the glassy surface of the water as
Molly ignored the valet parking and pulled her Toyota into a vacant space.

She realized only as she headed toward the blue
awning over the entrance that she was underdressed
for the place, and hoped that since it was barely five-
thirty, she was too early for most of the dinner crowd.
Looking down to brush at the wrinkles in her khaki
slacks as she passed through the first of two doors, she
collided head-on with Ben Boyd rushing out the interior door.

Reflexively, Ben raised his hands to Molly's upper
arms to stop her from the rebound of the collision. It
took a moment of mutual excuse-me's before they
recognized each other.

Molly instantly wondered what she was doing there,
and at the same time felt a slow sizzle under his hands.

"Molly?" Ben recovered first. "I was just on my
way to your house."

"Oh," she said dimly, wishing she hadn't come and
yet feeling a little thrill at the very sight of him.
"I...uh...I had to go to the store so I thought I'd just
stop by and tell you what Karen and I decided." It was
feeble, and she knew it.

"Look," he said with a glance back over his shoulder at the interior of his restaurant. He kept a hold on

her even though there was no more danger of her losing her balance. "Let me buy you a cup of coffee at Marie Callendar's next door. If I go back in my own place, there'll be a million interruptions."

"Oh," she said again, more dimly than the first time. "You don't have to do that. I just came to answer your questions. It'll only take a minute."

"No, I want to. I've been worrying about you all day. I wasn't on my way to see you because of the funeral details, I wanted to make sure you were okay." He finally let go of her arms only to take her elbow and turn her back around through the outer door.

"I really shouldn't. My sister and her kids moved in today, and I don't have any groceries and..." Then why had she come in the first place? she taunted herself. Shelter from the storm. "Well, maybe I can spare a few minutes."

It didn't seem to matter whether she agreed. He was taking her down the path to the more family-oriented Marie Callendar Restaurant, anyway.

The hostess there greeted him by name and immediately seated them in a secluded booth in a bar decorated with the coziness of a Victorian library.

"Two coffees, Paul," he called to the bartender before a waitress had a chance to ask.

"I drink tea," Molly said, feeling silly and thinking she should have just swallowed down the coffee even though she hated the stuff.

"I should have asked. Would you rather have a drink?"

"No, tea will be fine."

"Make it one coffee and one tea," he amended, and then settled his silver eyes on her. "Want to set me straight on the details of the funeral so we can get it over with and relax?''

She doubted that she would ever be able to relax with this man who had the oddest effect on her, but she pretended to go along with it, anyway. "The answer is no to all three—we don't want to view the body, and we don't want a family car or a procession. In fact I'm not even sure my sister will go to the service. She's . . . not up to it.''

"Because of the shock of your father's death?"

Their beverages came, giving Molly something to do with her hands. She felt much better unwrapping the tea bag and dunking it in the tiny silver pot than looking at Ben Boyd's finely honed features. "No, she left her husband today.''

"I see. That's why she's just moved in with you.''

"Yes, but the house is half hers, anyway. It belonged to our grandparents and was left to us both when they died.'' Why was she telling him all this?

"I'll be honest with you, John didn't give me much information about you or your sister. He had apparently kept tabs on you through a mutual friend, but he wasn't in any shape to recount your history.''

Molly interrupted him. "He kept track of Karen and me?'' she asked around the clog that seemed to form in her throat in response to every mention of her father. The fact that he had been in touch with someone who had reported on her made her feel . . . what? Uncomfortable? Hurt? Resentful? Unnerved? Angry that he hadn't kept in touch himself? And, she had to admit, slightly stirred to know that he must have cared, even just a little.

Ben put sugar in his coffee. His eyes didn't meet hers. "I had the feeling that he knew all about you.''

He took a drink of his coffee and went on with what he had been about to say when she had interrupted him. "Anyway, all day long I've wondered if I should have postponed things and waited to tell you at home tonight when you might have had someone around for comfort—a boyfriend or something."

He was obviously fishing. It pleased Molly unaccountably—a much better feeling than thoughts of her father left her with. "I don't have a boyfriend or something."

Ben grinned, showing straight, even teeth as white as the ducks on the pond. When he smiled, the deep indentations of his cheeks turned into long creases, and the corners of his remarkable eyes crinkled just slightly. It gave Molly heart palpitations.

"What about you?" she asked, hoping it sounded like plain small talk. "Are you married?"

"I've never had the pleasure."

Molly laughed cynically at that. "Funny, I've never thought of marriage as a pleasure. I don't think my sister would agree with that, either, at this point."

"Maybe she and her husband have just had a disagreement," he offered hopefully.

"No, her husband had an affair," she informed him curtly, though again she wondered at her own candor.

He frowned and shook his head. "I'm sorry," he said as if he really was. "And then all this with your father on top of it. You must both be overwhelmed."

That's why I'm here, she thought, but she merely shrugged. "Do you have family?"

Apparently the thought brought good feelings, because he smiled warmly. "A brother and two sisters."

"And your parents? Are they still living?"

"Yes." Then something seemed to strike him. "I don't know anything about your mother and I should have asked. Should she be included in the arrangements?"

Molly warmed her hands around her teacup, keeping her glance there rather than look at him. "My mother died when I was fifteen."

Ben closed his eyes. His unruly eyebrows arched high as he rubbed his forehead with the tips of just his index and second fingers. "I didn't know. John didn't say anything about her, and I . . . well . . . it didn't occur to me. He gave me such specific instructions about you and your sister that I just didn't think about anybody else."

"It's all right. She wouldn't have wanted to be included, anyway," Molly said sardonically.

A waitress refilled Ben's coffee cup, exchanging some good-natured gibes. When she had left, his gaze returned to Molly. "Are you a widow?"

That took her by surprise. "Am I a widow?" she repeated. "No, I've never been married."

"You haven't?" He seemed as surprised as she. "Then where did the Mercer come from?"

"My mother. When she took back her maiden name, my sister and I chose to take it, too."

He shook his head and spoke more to himself than to her, "Chalk another one up to wrong conclusions. I have to quit imagining these scenarios." Then he explained, "Since you were Mercer instead of Northrup, I assumed that was your married name. I . . . uh . . . noticed you didn't wear a wedding ring and you seemed to be in charge at Mercer Moving and Storage, so I thought you must be a widow running the business your husband left you."

"Mercer Moving and Storage was my grandfather's business. Karen and I inherited it from him."

"Your *maternal* grandfather?"

Molly was confused by the emphasis he put on that. "Yes, my maternal grandfather."

"John's in-laws. I see. That makes a little more sense," he said, once again to himself.

"I'm not following you."

"It doesn't matter. We'll get around to everything in time."

We'll get around to everything in time—did that mean they'd be seeing more of each other? Molly wished the simple comment didn't create such hope in her. She concentrated on the other part of what he had said. "What 'everything' will we get around to?"

"It's not important right now. After the funeral, when your life has calmed down, we'll talk."

She was disinclined to pursue it—and not because it gave her a reason to see more of Ben Boyd, she told herself. It was because she already had more to deal with than she could handle, and nothing to do with her father really mattered, anyway.

The restaurant was filling up, a sign to Molly that she had indulged herself all she could. "I'd better get going. I left Karen and my nieces napping, but I want to be there when they wake up."

"How much younger is your sister?" he asked instead of agreeing to her retreat. Then he added, "At least I assumed she was younger. I really am going to stop assuming things. I haven't gotten anything right yet. But your father said you were who I was to contact after his death, so I assumed you were the oldest."

"This time you were right. Karen is a year younger."

He grinned as if she had played right into his hand. "So how old is she?"

Molly laughed at that. "I'm thirty-three."

"Thirty-three," he repeated.

"Don't you approve?" she asked when he seemed to be doing mental calculations.

That brought him out of his reverie. He smiled at her again, his expression teasing. "I approve of everything about you."

Sizzle. Now even his words did it. Molly knew she had better get out of there. She took her purse off the seat beside her. "I really do have to go."

Ben tossed three dollars on the table and stood as she slid out of the booth. "I'd like it if you would let me pick you up and take you to the service tomorrow. Your sister, too, if she decides to go."

It was tempting. There was something so alluring about this man. Molly didn't understand it, but she knew enough to be leery. "Thanks, but things are too chaotic right now to say what I'll be doing by then. Besides, it really isn't a big deal."

Again he took her elbow as they left. For such a simple gesture it had an unnerving power over her. Warm currents radiated through her body again. It was at once exciting and comforting.

"Did the valet park you?"

"No, I did it myself."

"Lead the way, then."

He walked with her to her car, waiting while she unlocked the door. Then he opened it for her. "I feel better about letting you out of my sight now. You do finally seem all right."

"I am," Molly reassured him as she got in behind the steering wheel. Not in small part due to him, she realized.

Ben stepped into the L of the open door and leaned his arm along the top of the car to peer down at her. "I'm not convinced that you should drive yourself to the service tomorrow, though. Do you still have my numbers in case you decide to let me take you?"

"I have them. But don't plan on it." She suddenly felt reluctant to leave. This day was definitely crazy.

"My offer is still good if you decide you need someone to talk to . . . or whatever."

"Thanks." He seemed just as disinclined to let her go. When he stayed leaning against the car, she said, "I'd better get to the grocery store."

He stared at her for another moment, those silver-gray eyes of his piercing. Then he smiled just slightly and nodded. "Sure. I'll see you tomorrow."

Irrationally, she was disappointed when he finally did close the door. He pounded the hood lightly and stepped back out of the way.

Feeling like a teenager behind the wheel for the first time, Molly fumbled with her key, gave the car too much gas as she started it and ground the gears putting it into reverse. Still he stood watching her appreciatively and yet as if he was trying to figure something out.

Molly raised just her hand in a wave as she pulled away from the parking place. He waved back, but he didn't leave. In fact he stood watching until she could no longer see him in her rearview mirror.

Back into the fray, she thought as she waited for the light to turn green on Union Street.

But somehow she felt renewed enough to face it all again.

Chapter Three

Ben had just lathered his hair the next morning, his eyes shut tight against the sting of shampoo suds, when his shower turned ice cold.

It was an old trick he knew well.

"Damn you, Rick," he said as he felt for the faucet. Finding it, he turned the hot water back on and rinsed his head. Then he slammed the curtain back to find his brother leaning against the bathroom sink, arms crossed over a three-piece suit and a satisfied smirk on a face considerably rounder but nonetheless similar to Ben's. As he reached for his towel with one hand, he flicked water in Rick's direction with the other.

Rick ducked out of the bathroom, adeptly dodging the spray. "You sounded groggy on the phone. I just thought you needed a little pick-me-up."

"Thanks, pal. I sounded groggy on the phone because I was sleeping when you called. Not everybody gets up before the sun like you fishermen do. I don't suppose it occurred to you to just do like I said—let yourself in and have a cup of coffee if I was in the shower?" Ben only pretended to grouse.

"Coffee wasn't ready yet," Rick said over his shoulder as he headed toward a kitchen that was more like a cupboard and appliance-lined hallway.

Ben wrapped the towel around his waist, used another to dry his hair and then followed his brother.

While Ben poured the coffee, Rick picked up a paperback book from the countertop and read aloud. "*Preparing for Childbirth with the Lamaze Method.*" He raised an accusatory gaze to Ben. "You have something to tell me, little brother?"

"How about mind your own business?" Ben suggested as he handed Rick a mug.

"I'm your lawyer. Your business is my business, remember?"

"How are Tammi and the kids?" Ben asked instead of satisfying his brother's curiosity, knowing it was the best way to torment him.

"You had dinner with us night before last, remember? They're as fine as they were then. What gives with this Lamaze stuff?"

Ben gave him a smirk to match the one Rick had greeted him with and went around to the small living room. Newspapers, sports magazines, discarded clothes and shoes and various other debris littered the floor and furniture. Not seeming to notice, Ben cleared a spot and sat on the couch.

Obviously noticing and disapproving, Rick did likewise and sat on a low, overstuffed chair. "This place is a mess."

"Hey, not all of us are lucky enough to have a wife to pick up."

"I pick up after myself or catch holy hell."

"Well, then, you have incentive. I don't."

"So, what are you doing with a Lamaze book?" Rick persisted.

"Paula Brazos needs a coach."

Rick sobered. All brotherly teasing disappeared. "Oh, my God, is the baby yours?"

Ben laughed. "I have not been involved with Paula that way in over a year and a half, *Dad*."

"Then why are you her Lamaze coach?"

"Because we were friends who became lovers for a very brief time when we were both lonely, and then realized it was a mistake and went back to being friends. The creep that fathered the baby walked out on her when he found out she was pregnant. She needs a coach, and asked me to do it. No big deal."

"You really know how to blow a married man's fantasies of single life, don't you? You work longer hours than I do, you haven't had a vacation in three years, you live in a pigsty and now for kicks you're going to be the Lamaze coach for a woman having someone else's baby. Where are the hot young things in bikinis vying for the chance to do your laundry and clean your apartment? Where are the footloose trips to Vegas or the all-night poker parties or the week-long orgies or any of the things we married lugs imagine you single guys are out doing?"

"They're all in married lugs' imaginations," Ben said wryly. "I'm thirty-five years old. I did most of that stuff—well, not the orgies, but variations of most of that stuff—for a long time. Like everything, it gets old. Besides, you don't fool me. If single life was so great, how come you got married fresh out of college?''

Rick patted his paunch. ''Because you got all the good genes.''

''Because you found a woman you loved and were smart enough to grab her.''

Rick looked smug and raised an eyebrow lasciviously. ''Yeah, and I keep grabbing her every chance I get.''

''Lucky man.''

''I know. Maybe you should take another look at Paula. If you're good enough friends to be her Lamaze coach, could be there's enough there to build on. Tammi's my best friend.''

Ben shook his head. ''I told you, we tried that route, and it didn't work. There's no draw, no magnetic force, no chemistry, no fireworks...''

''You're drifting on me.'' Rick laughed. ''You look like someone out of an old black-and-white melodrama whose mind is wandering to the mystery woman he just bumped into in the street.''

Ben muttered, ''You'll never know how close you are to the truth,'' and took a drink of his coffee.

''Come on...'' Rick said in disbelief.

''Okay, so it isn't like in the movies. But there is a magnetic force.''

''Who with?''

''I feel like a ghoul saying it. Molly Mercer.''

''One of John Northrup's daughters?'' His disbelief grew.

Ben nodded. "It's incredible. I feel this pull that I've never felt before."

"So go for it. It'd be a great setup. You could keep your business in the family."

Ben rolled his eyes.

"No, really, what's holding you back? Is she married?"

"No, she's not married."

"Then what's the obstacle?"

"Her father, my friend and business partner has just died. What do I say? So, now that we've got your father buried, how about a date?"

"Okay, not many people get together romantically through a death. But that doesn't mean it can't happen. Where is there a rule that says you can't encounter the love of your life at a funeral?"

"It just doesn't feel right. She's John's daughter, and . . ." Ben shook his head, not really able to understand himself. "There's something else there, and I don't know what it is. Something between them that I don't understand. It's like all of a sudden I'm seeing shadowy images of John that just don't fit with the man I thought he was. Hell, you're going to think I'm crazy, but every now and then she says something that makes me feel like I should defend him, and I don't even know against what." He ran his hand through his hair in agitation. "Maybe I'm imagining things. Anyway, lusting after her just doesn't seem quite right."

"But you're lusting after her, anyway. Life does go on, you know. If I were you, I wouldn't let the fact that death has brought you together stand in your way. And as for her being your friend's daughter, I don't know what difference that should make. He liked you. He'd approve."

"Yeah, well . . . Want another cup of coffee?"

"Can't. I have an appointment." From his breast pocket Rick took an envelope and handed it to Ben. "Here you go. John's attorney in California forwarded it to me, I checked it out and everything is fine. Are you sure you don't want me to do this?"

"A formal reading of the will? I don't think so. I understood it when I read it. It's straightforward, uncomplicated. There's nothing in it but the partnership. Did you include one of your cards in case they have any questions?"

"Sure."

"You have more experience in this stuff than I do. When is the best time to give it to them? It doesn't seem right to just hand it over after the service at the graveside."

"That would definitely be bad form. I say hang on to it and give it to them a little later, after the emotions have had a chance to settle. But don't wait too long. They need to know what they've inherited." Rick stood, took his cup into the kitchen and then went to the front door. "And if I were you, I wouldn't let circumstances or some misplaced sense of loyalty stand in my way on the other front."

"So you've said—three times." Rather than get up and walk his brother out, Ben craned his head way back and spoke to the ceiling. "I'll just have to see how it goes. Thanks for bringing this by."

"Sure. See you later," Rick said as he let himself out.

When Ben had finished the last of his coffee, he hoisted himself off the couch and headed for the bedroom to dress. Regardless of the hesitation he had voiced to his brother, the attraction he felt for Molly

Mercer was too strong to ignore. There weren't many women like her around. Once this funeral was over, he had a built-in reason to see her and, strange circumstances or not, he had high hopes of getting to know this woman.

Rain clouds were a thing of the past that morning. The sun shone in a sky so clear and blue that it made it hard for Molly to believe so much gloomy disaster had struck just the day before. But it had, and though she wished it could all evaporate in the renewed heat of the last day of August, there was no such luck.

She had taken her two solemn-faced nieces to school, overhearing the venting of their own tensions as they bickered. But taking over the early-morning chore so her sister could rest had proved futile. By the time she got home, a swollen-faced Karen was sitting in the living room, staring into space as if she were in a trance.

"I was hoping you'd get a little sleep this morning," Molly greeted her as she closed the door from the garage into the house.

Karen turned her face up to Molly in slow motion. "I dreamed of Carl in bed with his assistant. Adrenaline kicked in, and I bolted out of bed as if the house were on fire."

"Yuck," Molly said, trying a little levity as she took off her sweatsuit jacket. It didn't work, Karen stayed morose. "Can I fix you a cup of coffee?"

That did work. Karen sort of half smiled, half grimaced. "You make coffee like mud, Molly, and right now I couldn't even drink the best coffee in the world."

"How about toast or something?"

Karen wrinkled her nose and shook her head. "Thanks, anyway. And thanks for getting the kids to school. How were they this morning?"

"Not their cheery selves. It'll do them good to be busy and away from things, get their minds off of this for a while."

Karen agreed with a nod. "I don't think I'm going to make it to the funeral," she admitted soberly.

"Good." Molly pulled off the rubber band that held her hair in a thick ponytail. "There isn't any reason for you to go. I was hoping you wouldn't push yourself."

"I feel a little guilty about it," Karen said softly, looking down at her lap where she was twisting a Kleenex into a tight corkscrew.

"Don't," Molly was quick to assure her. "Neither of us is obligated to go. I will, for the sake of...I don't know. Appearances, I guess. But there's no way you should. You have enough to deal with. You're in shock. It's ridiculous to even consider it." She slipped off her sweatpants, leaving only the nylon T-shirt she wore as pajamas. "I better get going. I have to call Nancy, and then take a bath and wash my hair before I leave."

"Go ahead," Karen said, falling over sideways on the couch, her feet still on the floor, and closing her eyes.

Molly used the phone in her pale blue bedroom rather than the one in the kitchen. She hadn't told Karen about Mercer Moving and Storage's latest catastrophe and she didn't want her to overhear.

When her secretary answered, Molly said, "Hi, Nance. It's just me. I wanted to check in and make sure the roofers had gotten there."

"A few minutes ago. Bruce is getting them started right now. How's it going on the home front?"

"Holding our own."

"How's Karen?"

"She's awful."

"Has she talked to Carl?"

"No, she doesn't want anything to do with him right now. I don't suppose it'll last."

"Now, Molly..." Nancy chastised.

"I know, I'm jaded. I'm trying to keep my big mouth shut. It's not easy, but I'm trying."

"Don't be jaded," her friend lectured. "I keep telling you to think of my Bill. He's a good man, and that proves there really are some of them out there. Concentrate on the positive, not the negative."

Instantly, a vivid picture of Ben Boyd popped into Molly's mind. Where had *that* come from? She pushed it aside. "I think Carl's affair takes him out of Bill's league. What do you think?"

"That you're a skeptic. But I'm not giving up. One of these days I'm going to change you. I suppose that hunk Ben Boyd will be at the services today?" Nancy said pointedly.

"I suppose so," Molly answered noncommittally.

"I liked him."

"Okay, I'll take Bill."

"I liked him for you."

I liked him for me, too. Molly pushed the thought away the same as she had the mental picture of him, reminding herself that she was better off alone. "He was friends with my father. What does that tell you?"

Nancy's voice sobered. "Nothing. That does not mean they were alike."

"My grandmother used to say show me who you go with, and I'll tell you what you are."

"No, no, no!" the secretary shrieked. "Don't write a guy like that off just because he knew your father."

"He didn't just know him. They were good friends of long standing."

"I certainly hope you're just being contrary. I know you do this—think you're protecting yourself by finding fault when you're attracted to a man. Just don't condemn him before you've had a chance to get to know him."

"I'll probably never see him again after this morning," Molly said, inwardly hoping it wasn't true, and at the same time wishing she didn't care if she ever saw him again. She'd gone insane. She knew it.

"*Arrange* to see him again," Nancy urged.

"I have to *arrange* a way to reimburse the Petrys for the water damage to their furniture. I don't have time to *arrange* anything else," she affectionately mocked her friend.

"Well, I've already put his card in the Rolodex. I'm not going to let you forget this guy."

"You're overlooking one minor point, Nance. No one said the man was interested."

"Are you nuts? You're too great-looking for any man not to be interested. Besides, I saw the expression on his face when he left your office yesterday."

Molly hated the little flutter her heart did. She hated herself for asking, "What expression was that?"

"The one Bill gets every time he remembers why he's wild for me. Of course Mr. Ben Boyd looked a little more serious and a lot less...uh...amorous, but then it was only the first time you'd met."

"You're imagining things."

"And you've been single too long. Everybody should try marriage at least once in her life, if only for the experience," Nancy lectured.

"Misery loves company," Molly countered, and then changed the subject. "I have to get going. Karen's in rotten shape, I don't know whether I can leave her alone here all day, or if I'll need to come back home this afternoon. I'll call around twelve and let you know if I'm going to make it in at all today."

The reminder of the other problems in Molly's life subdued Nancy's romantic enthusiasm. "Don't worry about anything around here. If we need you, I'll track you down." The secretary paused and then said, "I hope you really are as okay about this funeral as you say you are."

"I am," Molly assured her easily enough. "Hold down the fort while I'm gone, and I'll talk to you later."

Replacing the receiver in the cradle, Molly quickly made her four-poster bed, finishing it with two crocheted pillows that matched the tiny flowers in her blue bedspread. She gathered yesterday's clothes from where she had tossed them on a rocking chair and put them in the hamper. Then she took clean underwear from the tall antique bureau that stood beneath an oval mirror on the wall. Her purse was on top of the dresser, and it caught her attention.

Funny, but she could go literally years without even remembering that picture was in her wallet. And other times she was drawn to it for no particular reason at all.

Today she couldn't say she was drawn to it for no particular reason. It had been on her mind off and on since hearing about her father's death.

She might as well give in.

As she set her underclothes on the bureau top, her arms felt weighted and she reluctantly reached inside her purse for her billfold.

It was a nondescript taupe-colored clutch with compartments for change, for paper money, for her checkbook, for credit cards, driver's license, photographs. But this picture didn't have a slot there among those of her mother, her grandparents, Karen, Carl and the kids. It didn't have a place of honor, a place it might be glanced at easily or proudly shown. This picture was buried in the space behind the change purse where nothing was really supposed to go.

No one had ever known she had it. Not even Karen. Molly herself had always wondered why she kept it. Looking at it had never once made her feel good. It always made her sad. It always hurt.

And yet every now and then she was drawn to take it out and look at it, just as she did now.

The black-and-white picture was yellowed and frayed around the edges. It was a little blurry. They had always teased her mother about what a rotten photographer she was, and this was no exception. Molly remembered the day it had been taken. No special day. Just a rainy Saturday afternoon when she had been playing dress-up, like so many other days. Her family had been to a wedding a few weeks before, and it had inspired her to imitate the bride. This particular day she had done herself up so elaborately that her mother had laughed and said she had to have a picture of that.

So there stood eight-year-old Molly in that picture, decked out in a muddy white dress that drooped off of one shoulder to show her striped T-shirt underneath.

On her small feet were high-heeled shoes that looked gigantic, and turbaned around her head for a veil was a bath towel held in place with a headband worn like a tiara. Silly. But she remembered thinking at the time that she looked absolutely beautiful.

And there beside her in the picture stood her father, tall and straight, pretending to be very serious, giving the bride away.

Her hand was in the crook of his elbow. His much larger one was nearly covering it. For just a moment she remembered the feel of his hand over hers—big and warm. Protective.

Tears welled in Molly's eyes.

She also remembered the day she had found this picture—four years later while packing her things. She remembered thinking that her father had already given her away. For real.

Molly dropped her head back so no tears could fall. She swallowed hard.

To the ceiling, in a whisper, she said very snidely, "And you never could have me back...even if you had wanted me."

And then she put the picture back in her wallet and went to wash her hair.

It was a very small funeral, but after a person had been twenty-one years out of the state, and with only a single day's notice in the paper, Ben hadn't expected more.

Throughout the service he stood beside Molly, watching her out of the corner of his eye. Her clothes, he decided, were an indication of the conflict he sensed in her. She wore a sedate gray suit that was appropriate for the occasion, but beneath it was a red blouse and from the breast pocket spilled a red silk scarf. She stood very straight, very stoically. Her expression was blank. She did not shed a tear. She did not look, for even a second, as if she was attending the funeral of anyone closer to her than a business acquaintance.

Afterward Ben stood nearby as she accepted condolences perfunctorily and introduced him as her father's friend in a way that made it seem as if her function was to offer her support of him, instead of the other way around.

When everyone had left the graveside, she turned to Ben and in a matter-of-fact tone of voice said, "The service was very nice. Thank you for handling it. If you don't mind, I'd like some time alone here now."

"I'll wait for you by the cars," he offered, not wanting to leave her. Though it wasn't in evidence now, he remembered the vulnerability he had seen the day before, the shadow of a little girl lost. He knew it was still there, hidden behind her stoicism.

But Molly shook her head and said firmly, "No thanks. I really want to be by myself."

Still Ben stalled for time. "I have some papers of your father's that you need to see...."

That was as far as he got. She cut him off. "Not right now. I..." She drew a sharp, unexpected breath. "I have so much on my mind."

That stammer was the closest Ben had seen her come to cracking. *You're not as tough as you want me to think, Molly Mercer.* But what was he going to do? This was her father. She had a right to a final few minutes alone with him. And yet Ben had the strangest feeling that to leave her to herself today was to abandon her. "I could meet you back at your house, say, in an hour?"

She looked away from him, and he was sure she was fighting hard now to contain her emotions. The thought of what she must be feeling stabbed him.

When she spoke, her voice was choked. "Not now. I can't deal with papers now. Maybe tonight..."

She sounded so desperate to get rid of him. Wanting to help, to support, to comfort, he realized he was really only making it more difficult for her. He had to comply. "Tonight, then," he answered reluctantly, but for a moment he couldn't make himself move.

"Please," she whispered.

He reached for her, touching only her arm with one hand—a very proper, civilized comfort when what he really wanted to do was hold her so tight....

Then he sighed, squeezed her arm and let go. "If you need me..." But he didn't finish the sentence he had said so often to her in these past twenty-four hours. Instead he finally granted her her wish and left.

Once inside his car, parked in front of hers at the curb, he couldn't make himself drive away. Seeing her in the distance, he could tell she was crying at last. But it wasn't only grief that came flooding out of her. There was also the fiercest, most bitter anger he had ever been witness to in his life.

Though he could hear nothing, he could see that she was speaking to the casket, berating it. Ben felt as though he was intruding on a family argument. He shouldn't stay and watch something so obviously personal. She had a right to privacy.

But concern for her and curiosity kept him there.

He watched as she fumbled in her purse, took something from it and flung it at the coffin. That seemed to be the end of her tirade. She drew herself up straight and stiff again and walked several steps away from the gravesite.

But then she stopped. Standing very still, she appeared undecided for a moment before turning back.

Ben watched as she paused, let her head fall far forward as if in defeat, and then bent to pick up whatever it was she had thrown at her father's casket. Angrily she jammed it back into her purse and finally headed for her car.

Feeling as though he'd been caught spying, Ben at last started his own engine and slowly eased away from the curb. In his rearview mirror he kept an eye on her, making sure she was actually leaving.

They pulled out of the cemetery at nearly the same time, he turning left and she right. But long after she was out of sight, Ben couldn't help wondering just what was going on inside of Molly Mercer.

"Look, Carl, I'm trying not to get mad, but she doesn't want to see you." Molly stood like a sentry blocking the front door against her brother-in-law's entrance that night just after dark.

"I want to see them," Carl Dune insisted. "Whether Karen wants to see me or not I have a right to see my kids."

"You left your rights in bed with your assistant," Molly ground out through clenched teeth, barely noticing the car that stopped in front of her house.

"Mind your own business, Molly!" Carl shouted.

"I am. It's my business to pick up the pieces your libido left in the gutter!" she shouted back just as Ben Boyd got out of his car. The man had a knack for walking into the worst messes of her life. Then again, lately there wasn't anything in her life that wasn't a mess. And she was getting really tired of it.

She forced herself to speak more calmly. "Just back off for a while, Carl. The kids are upset. Karen's upset. Give them some breathing room for a couple of days. That's what you agreed to, remember?"

But Carl Dune didn't seem to notice that Ben had climbed the porch steps behind him. He still shouted. "I don't care what I agreed to, dammit! Let me in that house, or so help me God, I'll break in!"

"It's all right, Molly." Karen's voice came from behind her. "Let him in before he makes even more of a fool of himself for all the neighbors to see."

Molly looked from Ben Boyd to Carl and then back over her shoulder at her sister. What she really ought to do is just run away, she decided. "You don't have to talk to him, Karen," she said instead.

"It's okay." Her sister's voice sounded more angry than Molly's had. Molly took a deep breath and unlocked the screen door. Carl Dune stormed in, and she stepped out to face Ben Boyd.

He smiled ruefully. "Looks like my timing was bad."

She exploded. "These days there isn't a way to have good timing. Leaky roofs, water damage, no insurance, adulterers, death... My life is suddenly a soap opera!"

Ben smothered a sympathetic chuckle.

Molly wondered why he was there. Not that she wasn't glad to see him—pleasure at the sight of him seemed to be a reflex even in the midst of anger and frustration. Papers, she remembered suddenly. He had said something about some papers of her father's that he had to give to her. The thought didn't help her mood, and it must have shown in her expression.

"You look like you could use some fresh air. How about a walk?" he offered.

Last night he had been shelter from the storm. Tonight he was an open door to escape through. It was very tempting.

Molly glanced in the front window, wondering if she should stick around for moral support or protection or something. Ben must have guessed her doubts.

"I'll bet they know how to fight on their own."

"Okay," she agreed. "But on one condition."

"Name it."

"I don't want to hear anything but small talk. Not one word that makes any difference to anyone in the whole world. Not death or divorce or funerals or affairs or that the country's headed for another recession. Nothing. In fact, you can even save whatever papers you want to give me for another time because I don't care what's in them and I need a break!" she ended with a stifled shriek.

"Fair enough."

He stepped back to free the way down the porch steps and then followed her lead. As if by tacit agreement that Molly needed a few moments to calm down, neither of them spoke. They walked near, but didn't touch, he with his hands in the pockets of navy blue slacks, and she with hers jammed in the back pockets of her jeans.

The temperature was perfect, just cool enough to make the day's heat forgettable, and just warm enough to be comfortable in shirt sleeves. The air smelled of lawn and earth and leaves. Stars spotted a clear sky, and the distant sounds of enthusiastic cheers enlivened the night.

The park just one block over was alive with summer tournaments—softball, volleyball, tennis. Only the swimming pool was quiet and dark as Molly and Ben turned onto the path that wound through the playground equipment and around the baseball diamonds and the tennis courts.

"Do you play?" Ben broke the silence, stopping to watch a tennis match in progress.

"No, I don't," Molly said, continuing to walk, not even glancing in the direction of the court.

Ben caught up with her in two steps. "Still feeling contrary?" he guessed.

"No, actually I feel a hundred percent better," she answered in a perfectly normal tone.

"I'm surprised you don't play tennis. Your father was one of the best I've known. I thought he would've taught you."

The coldness was back in her voice. "My father is one of the subjects I don't want to hear a single word about tonight. Remember you agreed."

He cleared his throat. "Sorry."

It took several more minutes of silence for her to chase away the unwanted thoughts of her father. But she succeeded and made the next effort herself. "Didn't you have to work tonight?"

"By eight the crowd had thinned out. I have a good manager who can handle things when I'm away, and I'll go back later to do the receipts and close up."

"Mmm," she said because she couldn't think of anything else to say. She was becoming increasingly aware of Ben Boyd beside her. He was very tall. She liked that. He seemed to have a sense of humor. She liked that, too. He was patient and even-tempered, tolerant of her bad mood. And being near him made her skin feel charged. It made her feel very feminine—not something she could often allow herself as the boss of burly truckdrivers.

"What about you? Did you go in to work this afternoon?" he asked.

"No. I had to drive Karen to her doctor to have her blood pressure checked, and by then the kids needed to be picked up from school. Before I knew it, the day was gone."

"And I'll bet you felt guilty."

The unexpected truth is his remark made her laugh. "You're very perceptive."

"And you have a nice laugh."

That embarrassed her. "How did you know where I lived?"

"Uh . . . your father gave me the address," he said carefully.

"Of course." That made her think of the funeral. She had decided Frank and Nora Alt had been the informers her father had used to keep track of her and Karen. Frank was a distant cousin of her grandfather, and Nora had been an old friend of the Northrups—a foot in each camp, as it were. She had made the connection when she had seen them at the service today.

"Do you usually live in that big house all alone?" Ben's deep voice broke into her thoughts.

"Yes, since my grandfather died last winter." Molly sighed. "We don't seem to be able to stay away from bleak topics, do we?"

"Tell me some safe subjects."

Molly thought about it. It had been so long since she had been in a social situation with a man that she realized she had forgotten how to make conversation. "Talk about anything. Your favorite movies, your favorite foods, hobbies, your first girlfriend..." Where had that come from?

She hazarded a glance over at him, wondering if he had heard it as suggestively as she had. He was smiling.

"My first girlfriend was Peggy Simons. She had white-blond hair, a big space between her two front teeth and warts that looked like turtle shells all over her hands."

Molly laughed again and realized that it felt good— better than anything had in two days. It was somehow cleansing. "She sounds like a charmer, all right." She grimaced up at him and repeated, "Warts that looked like turtle shells?"

Ben shrugged. "I was seven. I thought it was exotic. And I happened to like turtles at the time."

They walked past a snack bar, and Ben bought them ice cream cones. Since the playground was deserted, they wandered there to sit on a wooden jungle gym.

"What about you?" he asked, propping his thigh on the platform so that he was facing her. "Who was your first love?"

"Real or imaginary?"

"You had a fantasy love life at an early age?" he teased.

"Sure."

The streetlights that lit the softball fields cast a dim glow over the play area. There were deep shadows in the angles of his face, making him look all the more handsome. Molly was too aware of it. She looked out into the distance as she spoke.

"Movies and TV provided a wealth of fantasies. I had big crushes on several stars. I'd spend my allowances on movie magazines and hide them under my bed."

She could feel his glance on her. From under her brows she peeked up to find him staring intently.

"I would never have guessed that about you. You seem so practical."

She felt slightly insulted. "It was a long time ago before dreams were dashed."

He cupped her chin in his hand and turned her face to his. "That sounded very sad. I'd hate to think any of your dreams were ever dashed," he said sincerely.

Molly suddenly found it very difficult to swallow. His hair fell slightly across his forehead. His eyes were warm as he looked down into hers. She shrugged and in the process managed to extract her face from his grip. She was sizzling again, and she decided she had better drop the remainder of her ice cream in the trash before it started to boil in her hand. Besides, it gave her an excuse to move.

It was purely by accident that when she sat back down, she brushed against his shin propped on the platform.

Ben finished his own ice cream without moving his leg from where it touched her side. "And what about your real-life first love?"

"George Pancratson. Everybody called him George Pancreas, of course. He was nearly a foot shorter than I, at least twenty pounds lighter. He wore his hair slicked back and buttoned his shirts all the way to the throat."

Quite naturally, Ben took her hand and started to walk again, keeping hold of it as they wandered into a darker section of the path, the moon and lamplight dimmed by elm trees that formed an arch overhead.

The skin of his hand was a little rough and slightly callused. Seeming to fit as perfectly around hers as if it was meant to be there, it felt too good to balk at, so Molly ignored the warning alarms ringing in her brain and let it be.

When the only sound seemed to be the increased beat of her heart, she blurted out, "First kiss."

Ben pulled her nearer, holding her hand in both of his as they walked. He looked up into the tree tops as if remembering fondly. "It was very romantic. I was twelve and in first lust with my thirteen-year-old cousin. We were swimming in the pond at my folks' place, horsing around the way kids do when they're too self-conscious. I planted a big one on her, missed, jammed my chin into her nose and broke it."

Molly laughed. "Your chin or her nose?"

"Her nose. It's still a little crooked, and to this day she is not overly nice to me when we meet."

The path forked to either side of a massive tree, but instead of going around it, Ben stopped there. He leaned them both against the trunk, arching one arm up over Molly's head as he remained holding her hand with the other, keeping her close. His deep baritone voice was low, intimate. "What about yours?"

Molly's skin was alive, her head was light. She felt as carefree as kids are supposed to feel but rarely do. "Noses must be a common theme in first kisses," she said, hoping that by talking she could keep these feelings at bay.

From above, he reached down to run his index finger down the length of her nose. "I didn't notice any bumps on yours."

His touch left a tingling sensation that made her throat constrict in a purely pleasurable way. No doubt about it. This was definitely crazy. She didn't even really know this man.

"Your first kiss," he prompted when she didn't say anything.

"George Pancratson again. I was in third grade, and even love at that age doesn't allow for the mushy stuff. He followed me home from school, kissed me and I punched him in the nose. It bled all over one of those button-up shirts of his, and love turned licketysplit into hate. He tormented me for weeks afterward, saying that he was going to get even, that he knew karate and when I least expected it he was going to get me back. I couldn't sleep nights worrying about it. Every day he'd menace me with threats until I made a bargain with him. It cost me my lunch money for a solid week just to get him to leave me alone."

"I hope you learned a valuable lesson," Ben said in a husky voice, fingering her hair.

"You bet. Just how fine is the line between love and hate." He smelled of a tangy after-shave, and she was thinking more about that than what he was saying.

"I was hoping the lesson was along the line of learning to give in and enjoy it when a man kisses you."

"George Pancratson was a long way from a man." Why was her own voice so soft and breathy?

Ben let go of her hand and tipped her face up to his with the curve of one finger. He lowered his mouth to hers slowly, that first contact soft and nebulous, his breath a warm whisper against her skin. Then his kiss deepened tentatively, as if he was waiting for her to pull away. When she didn't, his arms came around her, pulling her close, one hand cupping the back of her head, holding her against the increasing pressure of lips that were only slightly moist and tasted sweet.

Molly let herself be carried away by the kiss. It had been a long, long time, and she was particularly vulnerable today. She closed her eyes and let her hands slide up to press his chest, finding it hard and strong beneath the coolness of his shirt. His lips parted, and hers seemed to follow suit all on their own as she relaxed into his embrace, into the feel of giving herself up to the powerful force that had been pulling them together from the very first.

Molly wanted it to go on and on. But the sound of another couple's conversation announced their approach. Those same hands that had reveled a moment before in the feel of his powerful chest pushed Ben away.

"Are you going to punch me in the nose now?" he asked with amusement, his arms still around her, though not holding her close any longer.

Looking him square in the chest, Molly shook her head in bewilderment, took a deep breath and said to herself, "What am I doing?" Then she jerked her head back up to find him watching her intently. "I have to get home and see how my sister is," she said in a rush.

He didn't let go of her until she stepped back. "Molly?" he asked.

This was her own fault. She was the one that had initiated the flirting. "I'm not myself today," she said by way of explanation as she started in the direction of her house.

Ben was beside her in an instant, but he didn't touch her. "Yourself doesn't kiss?" he tried, teasing her.

But Molly missed it. "No," she answered forcefully.

Ben stifled a laugh. "I'd like to amend that."

But Molly was too lost in her silent reprimand. How could she, in the midst of Karen's marital problems and the reminder of all her father had done, even begin to be attracted to any man? Let alone be swept off her feet by one. And with just one kiss.

"I want to see you again, Molly," Ben said as they climbed the steps of her front porch.

Her heart did a somersault, but her head sounded alarms. "I don't have time for dating." But rather than look at that face that did such strange things to her pulse, she pretended to try to see through the curtains of the front window into the house.

"We'll be seeing each other, anyway. But it's important to me that you know I want pleasure as well as business."

What was he talking about? She must have missed something. She forced herself to look at him in hopes that she might understand.

But there was nothing in that gorgeous chiseled face to give her a clue.

Ben took a folded envelope out of his back pocket and handed it to her. "I hate to end this on a bleak note when the last hour has been so nice. But this is the reason I came over tonight. It's your father's will. You and your sister need to read it, and then we have to talk."

Molly shook her head, her brain felt foggy. "I don't want anything that belonged to him."

"Just read it. And remember that totally separate from this, I want to get to know you."

"I can't handle any more complications in my life right now," she blurted out.

His smile was kind, warm, heart stopping. "I promise not to be a complication."

Then, before she realized what he was doing, he took hold of her upper arms and pulled her into another kiss, briefly, lightly, just enough to remind her of how much she liked it.

"I'll be in touch."

He left her standing there, holding the envelope in numb fingers, staring at his broad back as he crossed the lawn to his car parked out on the curb.

Her throat and chest were tight with tension, but her stomach was tight with something else entirely.

How could she have let the shelter become the storm?

Chapter Four

"We own forty percent of Boyd's Restaurants." In a tone of astonishment, Molly announced this to her sister when she had finished reading the will the following morning over breakfast.

Karen looked up from the cup of coffee she had been staring morosely into as if Molly were speaking a foreign language. "What?"

"The will." Molly rattled the paper she held in her hand for emphasis. "I told you about it last night after Carl left, remember?"

"No, I don't. I can't be expected to remember anything about that. Last night Carl threatened to not give me a dime as long as I refuse to go home now that he's changed his mind about our agreement for time out."

Molly was rereading the passage about the ownership of Boyd's restaurants, her nose nearly pressed to the second sheet of paper on the table in front of her. What she couldn't believe was that a cloud could actually have a silver lining. "I knew he would try to force you to go back," she said to Karen as she read. "And money is always the weapon of choice. That's why I told you to clean out your savings account yesterday."

"I just didn't think Carl would be like this."

Molly thought it prudent not to comment. "Did you hear what I said about this inheritance?" she said instead, satisfied that she really had read it right the first time.

"No," Karen sniffled, closed her swollen eyes and laid her head on the table beside her mug.

"Will you listen now? This is important," Molly insisted.

Karen looked up and stared forlornly at her sister. "Okay, I'm listening."

"If I understand this will, our father owned forty percent in Boyd's Restaurants and he left it to be split evenly between you and me."

"Does that mean I'll have money for the girls' school lunches when I've used up what's in my purse?"

Molly shook her head fatalistically. "You didn't take the money out of your savings, did you?"

Karen's eyes filled. "It seemed so underhanded. I told you I didn't think he'd be like this. I don't even have the checkbook. All I have is what's in my purse— about nineteen dollars." She sat up again, looking even more defeated upright than she had with her head on the table. "I know things are tight at the warehouse and I haven't minded not taking a profit-sharing check since Christmas. After all, you're doing all the work and hardly taking a thing. But under the circumstances can I pull anything out now?''

Molly stood and went to the sink to rinse the kids' cereal bowls and put them in the dishwasher. She didn't look at her sister when she finally answered. "I didn't want to tell you this because you have enough on your mind, and it's my problem, anyway." She recounted Mercer Moving's insurance woes. "Of course we can take what we need for groceries, utilities, the kids, anything that's an absolute necessity. But I can't say I'll bring you home a profit-sharing check this afternoon, because the truth is there aren't any profits to share."

"Oh, God," Karen moaned, closed her eyes and laid her head back on the table.

"It'll be okay," Molly reassured her, coming to sit down again now that the cat was out of the bag. She patted the papers on the table. "This inheritance just might be the answer to our problems. Maybe this is fate's hand in restitution."

Karen frowned in confusion, but didn't open her eyes.

Molly explained. "Look, I don't know what this is worth, but there are three Boyd's Restaurants. If we can sell our forty percent and sink it into Mercer Moving and Storage—pay off the Petrys, rebuild the engine on Number Three, maybe even buy a couple of new trucks, a new warehouse, who knows..."

Molly tried to contain her newfound enthusiasm. She was suddenly too energized to sit still. She got up and poured Karen another cup of coffee, talking fast as she did. "We can breathe new life back into the company. We might even get it to where it was before Grandma got sick, back to where we need it to be. Oh, we'll never get rich, we're too small for that. But we'll be independent, in control, secure all on our own. Then no one can take anything away from us, no one can hurt us. You won't have to worry about whether Carl comes through with support money."

When Molly looked over at her sister again, it was to find Karen sitting up and staring at her as if Karen were seeing her for the first time. "All those speeches of Mama's are still right there in the front of your mind, aren't they?" Karen whispered in a croaked voice. "Everything she used to say about a woman being self-sufficient, totally independent, not relying on anyone but herself, about making her own security and not trusting anyone else for it."

Molly shrugged and admitted without sounding defensive or judgmental. "She was right."

Karen gave a sad little laugh. "As I'm learning the hard way right now. I just never realized it was all so deeply ingrained in you."

Molly shrugged again and busied herself straightening the papers of the will, once more not looking at her sister. "That's why it's so important to save Mercer Moving and Storage. That and the fact that Grandpa built it and loved it." She could still feel her sister's gaze on her.

"I always wondered why you didn't use your business degree to do something else, something more chic than Grandpa's moving and storage company. But this is why, isn't it? It's the feeling of being in control of your own life, your own destiny."

For the third time, Molly shrugged, but then she looked her sister in the eye. "It's for you, too, Karen. Mercer Moving and Storage is half yours."

Karen groaned and grimaced and laughed while she shook her head. "Geez, that makes me feel guilty. All this time you've been worrying and working for that, while I sat in my little nest and never gave anything Mama said a second thought. And now here I am, staking a claim to half of it because I'm in just the boat you're killing yourself to stay out of."

Molly was pleased to see her sister come out of her own misery for just a moment and reclaim even a shred of her sense of humor. "Yep, you're lower than dirt," she teasingly agreed.

"So, that's what you want to do—sell out of Boyd's Restaurants."

"It seems like a godsend to me. Besides, I don't know anything about the restaurant business."

"I don't know anything about the moving and storage business, but that doesn't keep me from cashing profit-sharing checks. But I'll go along with whatever you think is best."

"I think it's best to keep all our eggs in our own basket."

"As Mama also used to say," Karen finished, "so what do you suppose we do about this? Or I should say what are you going to do about it? Even though I feel guilty not being involved, I don't have the faintest idea about business even on my best days, and these are a long way from my best days. I keep falling into some kind of conscious coma I don't think would be much good to you."

"The first thing I'll need to do is talk to Ben Boyd." A slight tremor ran down her spine at the thought.

"He's the old friend, right?"

"And the Boyd that Boyd's Restaurants are named after."

Karen nodded, waved her hand as if she were shooing flies and once more rested her head on the table. "Whatever. I trust you." Then she sighed and said, "Do you think I should call a lawyer?"

Molly laughed sadly. "Your mind does seem to wander. That's up to you, kiddo. Maybe you ought to think about it for a day or two. I'm going upstairs to call Ben Boyd before I leave."

Karen only groaned in answer as Molly left.

There was absolutely no reason in the world she needed to go upstairs into her own bedroom and securely close her door in order to make a purely business phone call to Ben Boyd. And Molly knew it.

So why the urge for privacy? Why didn't she just use the telephone in the kitchen?

She had an answer for it, but she didn't like it.

Since the moment he had left her standing on the front porch last night, she had not been able to get him completely out of her mind. Oh, she could manage for short spans of time. But only short ones. And then there he'd be again, popping up over and over like ducks in a shooting gallery.

She hadn't had more than a couple of hours sleep all night. Who could sleep being haunted with images of those steel-colored eyes? Of that handsome face? Of that big body? Of that deep voice? Of that kiss...

"I'm not doing much better than Karen in the drifting-off department," Molly mumbled to herself, taking from her purse the slip of paper on which she had written his numbers. As she began to dial, she was thinking that she was beginning to feel like some love-starved... "Love-starved?" she said aloud in answer to her own thoughts. "Oh, that's awful."

Just then Ben answered, his voice thick with sleep. Molly grimaced and had the urge to hang up. But when he repeated his hello, she decided to tough it through.

"I'm sorry if I woke you." Instantly she pictured him in bed, tousled and lazy and so relaxed. What did he sleep in? Pajamas? That wasn't how she saw him. Just his shorts? Good grief, what was she thinking?

"Molly? Is that you?"

It gave her an inordinate thrill that he recognized her voice. With a start she realized what she had to do. Severing all connections with Ben Boyd would stop this ridiculous reaction she had to him. "I didn't think you'd still be asleep."

She heard him fumble for something. "It's only eight thirty-four," he grumbled. "I did closing last night after I left you."

For some reason it embarrassed her for him even to mention that they had been together last night. It inspired too vivid a memory of his kiss. But he wouldn't be thinking the same thing, she consoled herself. "Sorry. It just didn't occur to me that I'd wake you."

"S'all right," he said, and then cleared his throat to guess at the reason for her call. "You read the will."

"This morning," she confirmed. "I need to discuss it with you."

"Great. I'd like to see you."

He sounded so genuinely happy about it. Warmth rushed through Molly. *Remember he's your father's friend. Show me who you go with and I'll tell you what you are.*

Her voice came out very businesslike then, pleasing her. Under the circumstances it seemed like a victory. "I'm swamped today, but if you wouldn't mind, I could come to your office . . . that is if you have an office . . . at your convenience after work.''

"Hmm. . ." He seemed to think about it. "I do have an office—three of them, in fact. But I'll tell you what, I was going to sneak over to that new restaurant on West Colfax for dinner—my favorite hobby is checking out the competition—and I'd love some company. How about it?''

"Dinner," she repeated dubiously, at first trying to think of a plausible excuse since she was the one who had initiated this. But then she reminded herself that if he was checking out the competition, he was actually working and she was only doing what she said she would—meeting him at his convenience during his work hours. "All right," she conceded.

"Terrific.''

He was talking then, and she had to force herself to concentrate on what he was saying rather than the timbre of his voice that somehow seemed like the sexiest thing she had ever heard.

"I'll pick you up. . . .''

Molly gained control of herself just in time to interrupt him. "No," she said too firmly. "I'll meet you. What's the name of the place?''

"Churchill's, but I would really like to pick you up.''

"I have a lot to do. I'll probably be out and about up until the time we meet," she lied. Not only was the thought of being in a closed car with him all too appealing, but this way he would realize this dinner was definitely a business meeting, not a date.

When he sounded disappointed, she realized it echoed a feeling of her own that she was trying to ignore. "Whatever you say, then. How is seven o'clock for you?"

Five would have been better. Seven seemed like a date, but she agreed, anyway.

"How are you doing this morning?" he asked, seeming reluctant to let her go.

"Good, thanks. Again, I apologize for waking you," she said in a rush to hide from these bizarre feelings.

"No problem. How about your sister?"

"She's as okay as anyone can expect, I suppose. She won't be coming with me tonight." Why had she said that, for crying out loud?

"Good," he answered without missing a beat. "I'd like to meet her sometime soon, but having dinner alone with you tonight is definitely preferable to seeing you in a crowd."

There was that sizzle again. "I have to get to work," she said in a near-panicked tone of voice. "Seven tonight at Churchill's. See you then."

Only after she had hung up did she realize she hadn't even given him the chance to say goodbye. She closed her eyes and shook her head. She hadn't acted like this as a teenager, and here she was doing it now.

"Get a grip on yourself, Mercer," she said sternly.

And then Molly left her room, feeling oddly as if she had just done something very intimate behind that closed door.

"I don't know what that smell is, but I hope it's what we're having for lunch," Rick Boyd announced as he walked into Ben's office in the Cherry Creek location of Boyd's Restaurant.

Since Ben's main office was in the Union Street eatery, this one was no more than a desk, a few filing cabinets and a dart board in a space off the storage room. Ben looked up from the ledger he was working on as his brother propped one hip on the edge of the desk. "You smell sautéed onions for the Philly sandwiches. You can have whatever you want—I told you it's the payback for looking over John's will for me."

"Then I want a big T-bone steak with the onions on the side."

Ben stood, patting his brother's paunch as he passed him on the way to the filing cabinet. "Want the works, too? Salad, baked potato..."

"And a beer. It's back to being summer outside, in case you haven't noticed."

"I hope this isn't what you usually eat for lunch." Ben relished giving his brother a hard time.

"Hey, you're getting off cheap—I bill out at a hundred an hour."

"Yeah, but that's only to people who haven't seen you with a runny nose and chicken pox. Come on, I'll put your order in on the way through the kitchen and we can sit out at the bar."

The decor of Boyd's East was that of an old gold mine, rustic and dimly lit. Shovels and picks hung from the walls, passageways were squared off with beams so they looked like shafts. It was furnished with Victorian pieces and lit with Tiffany lamps.

Because it was lunchtime, the bar was sparsely populated. Ben and Rick took two stools at the end.

"So how'd it go?" Rick asked as he poured his beer into a frosty glass.

"The funeral was fine. I gave Molly the will later that night."

"Molly?" Rick mimicked. "That sounded very familiar."

"We are, after all, partners now."

"You mean in business?" Rick raised a taunting brow.

"No, in crime."

"Could be partners in pleasure."

"You and Tammi and the kids going up to the folks' place over the weekend for Labor Day?"

"Very subtle, Ben. Very subtle." But Rick conceded to the change in subject. "Of course. Mom would have a fit if we didn't all show up. Why don't you invite your new *partner* to come. You know how Mom and Dad like a crowd."

"I also know that you're so nosey you're dying to get a look at this lady."

"I'm always dying to get a look at your ladies. I told you, I live vicariously. It's good for my marriage. Either they're so great they make me feel inferior but give me food for fantasy, or they make me soooo happy not to be in your shoes—like that airhead you brought up for the Fourth last year. Great body, but I figured you had to tie her shoes for her."

"You're as funny as a crutch, you know?"

"So, seriously, what do you think is going to happen with these new partners of yours? Your friend John stayed out of things, but there's no guarantee his daughters will."

Ben took a drink from the soda water he was nursing. Since meeting Molly, he hadn't even thought about the possibility of interference. It had occurred to him when John had first told him about the fact that his daughters would be inheriting the forty percent of Boyd's Restaurants. But meeting Molly had made him forget his concerns in favor of other thoughts. In fact, thinking of the woman as anything but a business partner seemed to have become his main occupation.

"I don't think John's daughters will want to come in and take over," Ben told his brother.

"They couldn't take over with forty percent, but they could make your life pretty miserable."

The thought of Molly in his life did not provoke a miserable image. Instead it gave him quite a rush. He didn't know why she seemed so resistant to this attraction between them, but partnership was a built-in requirement that they stay in contact. For that he would even accept a little interference.

"Have you thought of buying them out?" Rick asked, breaking into his preoccupation.

Ben stared at his brother for a moment, consciously pulling himself out of his reverie. "No," he said emphatically.

"Well, you might. Buying them out could save you a lot of headaches."

"I can't," Ben answered him curtly.

Rick drew back on his bar stool as if evading a punch. "Did I touch a raw nerve for some reason?"

Ben shook his head ruefully. "It just isn't that cut-and-dried. There's more involved than what's on paper."

"And obviously you don't want to let me in on it. So as your legal adviser, let me tell you that anything that isn't on paper isn't really valid."

"It's valid to me," Ben cut him off.

"Okay, okay." Rick raised his palms to ward off his brother again. "But for the record, I say think about pulling that forty percent back in."

* * *

So much for being out and about, Molly thought as she realized she was going to have to speed up her dressing in order to be there at seven. She had left work an hour early, come straight home and spent the past two hours getting ready.

But not for Ben, she steadfastly told herself. The past few days had been so tough that she had earned a couple of hours of pampering. But why not? Ben Boyd didn't have to know her toenails were now perfectly painted or that she didn't ordinarily wear eye shadow. These were just morale boosters.

Okay, so she was kidding herself, Molly thought as she tucked her cream-colored silk shirt into her linen pants and gave her hair a final fluff. But to admit the truth made her very, very uncomfortable.

She was a sworn and avowed independent woman and sworn and avowed independent women did not spend two hours primping to meet a man. They did not have a rapid pulse over the thought of seeing a man again. They did not have butterflies in their stomachs—and worse yet, lower—at the thought of a man. They did not debate with themselves over what they were going to wear. They did not borrow eye shadow to highlight their eyes, or try out a seductive new hairstyle. They certainly did not feel light-headed and so excited they thought they might faint as they walked out the door.

So Molly denied it all and felt better.

Churchill's parking lot was only moderately filled when she pulled into it. She could see Ben waiting outside the front doors, and goose flesh cropped up all along her arms. She ignored it.

"Remember, this is business," she said to herself as she locked her car. She slipped the long strap of her brown leather purse over her shoulder and walked toward him with a measured step to hide how really eager she felt. It was definitely a good thing that this meeting would set the wheels in motion to sever all connections with Ben Boyd. She must be allergic to him. Allergies, she had read in a magazine just the day before, could make children behave very strangely. She just assumed it could make adults do the same thing.

"You look terrific," he said in greeting as she approached him, his steel-colored gaze taking her in top to bottom to top again.

Her heart fluttered. It had nothing to do with the compliment—no matter how genuine it had sounded. And it had nothing to do with the fact that he looked wonderful dressed in charcoal slacks and a dove-gray shirt, the cuffs rolled to midforearm to expose those thick, masculine wrists of his and the gold watch that glimmered in the evening sunshine. Sworn and avowed independent women were not moved by things like that. It was just this allergy she had.

"Thank you," she said a little too brightly. She then cleared her throat and tried for a more businesslike tone. "I hope I didn't keep you waiting long."

"I made sure to be here early so you wouldn't have to wait for me," he said as he held the door open for her.

Passing in front of him to enter the restaurant, Molly caught a whiff of his after-shave—fresh, clean, piney. The scent was subtle and yet very heady. *So what am I supposed to do? Stop breathing?* she silently defended herself.

Churchill's was not crowded. Dimly lit and decorated in dark wood and leather and a tooled-copper ceiling, it reminded Molly of a den in an old English mansion. The atmosphere was a little more intimate than she would have chosen, which meant that were this a date, it would have been very cozy.

Requested by Ben, the maître d' seated them at a corner table from which Ben could see the bar and kitchen doors. It made Molly feel a world better to realize that he actually was here to check out the competition. It also disappointed her a little.

The menu was not large—London broil, Yorkshire pudding, and kippers along with the steaks and seafood that made it Boyd's competitor. While Molly studied it, she could feel Ben studying her.

"This is probably going to sound like an overused line, but I haven't been able to think about anything all day except seeing you again."

Me either was the first thing that popped into Molly's mind. She contained it and said, "That must have made for an unproductive day." Then she looked up from her menu to see him smiling as if he found her very funny.

"You're a fighter, I can see that. What I wonder is why you're fighting this so hard."

"Fighting what?"

His smile turned compassionate. "Us. This magnetic pull between us."

She studied the menu again. "The prime rib looks good."

He took the menu out of her hands. "I'm going to order one of everything," he said to both Molly and the waitress who had just come to their table. Ben seemed unaware of the surprise on both women's faces. After the waitress had garnered the details and left, he leaned back in his chair and explained himself to Molly. "How else am I going to check them out? Maybe their beef is good, but their fish is foul. Maybe they use decent quality ingredients in the inexpensive stuff and skimp on the gourmet. Maybe their portions are generous on the chicken dishes and scanty on the beef. Could be their chef is great with sauces to hide the fact that he mutilates the meat underneath. If I taste everything, then I know whether I should be envious of their chef or glad the meat mutilator is theirs and not mine. See?"

Molly laughed. "I see. What about the bartender?"

Ben shrugged. "I already know him. Wouldn't hire him. He waters the drinks. But we could have wine," he finished with an insinuating raise of one of those unruly eyebrows of his.

Again Molly couldn't help herself. She laughed and at the same time loosened up. "One glass of everything they offer?"

"That's better. I like to see you smile," he answered her expression in an intimate tone, then addressed her question. "No, the vagaries of wines are more a matter of record according to country, vineyard, year and crop—unless of course you're worried about someone sticking a dirty finger in it. If so I could uncork the bottle right here and pour while you watch," he teased.

"I need a clear head to discuss business. I think I'll just have iced tea—and don't tell me about the vagaries of iced tea because I won't buy that one."

Ben grinned mischievously at her. "Fresh brewed or instant, orange pekoe, English, Chinese, herbal or spiced. Say uncle and I'll give up shop talk."

"Uncle, uncle."

"Ah, too bad, and before I got around to coffees—espresso, cappuccino or Columbian blend."

"Want to hear about tire rotation, emission tests and crank shafts?" she threatened.

He ordered her tea and then stared at her for a moment, his gaze warm. "I'd rather hear about you."

Molly put her napkin in her lap and hoped the light was too dim to show any sign of the discomfort she felt beneath his concentrated interest. "That's really too boring to talk about."

"No, it really isn't," he assured her.

"We came to discuss my inheritance," she reminded him as two busboys set another table beside theirs to hold all of the meals the waitress was about to bring out.

"Do we have to?"

"Of course. That's why we're here."

"I thought we were here to have dinner and get to know each other better."

That was absolutely the last thing Molly wanted. "Karen and I were both shocked to find we inherited part of your restaurants," she said, firmly turning the conversation to what she had come to discuss in the first place.

With his glance still steadily on her and warmly familiar, Ben conceded to her change of subject. "Yes, I suppose you were. He owned one of his own in San Diego. In its last incarnation it was called The Gas Grill. But after he'd been sick awhile, he couldn't continue to run it. And, on top of being incapacitated, he needed the money for medical expenses, so he sold it.''

"The letter from his lawyer explained that, and that the only thing left of his estate after the last of the medical bills were paid was the forty percent of your restaurants. That's what I want to talk to you about.''

But the arrival of a dozen meals delayed that. When they were both settled with plates full of samples of everything that looked interesting, Molly broached it bluntly. "Karen and I want to sell our portion of Boyd's restaurants.''

Ben didn't seem surprised. He merely finished chewing the bite of steak he had just taken and took a sip of his wine. "Why?'' he asked simply enough.

Now Molly was on firm, familiar terrain. Her confidence was strengthening. "First of all, let me say that Karen has put this completely in my hands. Not only is she in no shape to deal with it, but even in the best of times she isn't interested in business. Since I handle all of that for us both, it's up to me. I don't know diddly about the restaurant business, so it's ludicrous for me to represent Karen and myself as partners in yours. Nor do I have any interest in learning it. Mercer Moving and Storage is what supports us, what I am devoted to seeing succeed. Frankly, we need the money.'' Molly explained the insurance problems. "So you see, selling out of your restaurants so we can put the money into Mercer Moving and Storage is an answer to our prayers.''

Ben sampled from those dishes he hadn't yet tried. "I'm sorry,'' he said.

Molly took it to be an offer of sympathy for her present hard times. "Thanks, but you can see that everything will be all right now that we'll have money from selling our inheritance.''

"No, I meant I'm sorry, but you can't sell your inheritance. Not that I'm not sorry for your company's bad luck. But I can't help you out with it.''

Molly put her fork down and stared at him. Maybe he just didn't hear well in the dark. "I don't think you understand. I fully intend to sell the forty percent ownership of your restaurants.''

Ben settled back in his seat and sipped his wine. "You can't.''

"What do you mean I can't?''

"Did you read the partnership agreement I gave you with the will?''

"I skimmed it.''

"Did you read the part that stipulated irrevocably that your forty percent cannot be sold to anyone but me?''

Molly was sitting very straight and stiff by this time. "No, I didn't,'' she admitted.

"It's a clause protecting me from that forty percent being sold to just anybody. I liked John, we worked well together, but more than that we had an understanding about the working arrangements of my restaurants. His initial investment was to help me get started. I could have bought him out a long time ago, but since he had nothing to do with the day-to-day running of Boyd's and never interfered in anything, I decided it didn't really matter.''

"If you could have bought him out a long time ago, then you shouldn't have any problems buying us out now,'' Molly reasoned persistently.

"I'm sorry,'' he repeated.

"Why?" she said too loudly, and then looked around to see if any of the other diners were staring. They weren't. Molly took a deep breath and lowered her voice. "Why in the world wouldn't you buy us out?"

Ben's mood seemed to have sobered. He frowned and ran his index finger around the rim of his wine glass. "There are a lot of things about your father's past and his relationship with you that I don't understand. But he apparently knew Mercer Moving and Storage was not in the pink and he foresaw your wanting to invest what he left you in it. This made more sense to me when I learned that Mercer Moving and Storage was your maternal grandfather's company. John was emphatic about wanting to leave you a legacy all his own."

"Don't be melodramatic," Molly berated. Tension was building in her.

"The words were his, not mine. A legacy of his own. He stressed that. Apparently he didn't want what he left you to be swallowed up into his ex-in-law's business. I guess that's understandable."

"To you, maybe, but not to me."

"He made me promise him that I would not buy you out unless it was in your best interests and never if the money was to be used for Mercer Moving and Storage."

"You tricked me," Molly accused, her tone echoing with disillusionment. "You asked me why I wanted to sell out, and like a naive jerk I told you. I should have known better than to trust anyone who was associated with my father."

Ben's gaze raised to Molly, his eyes hidden in the shadow of a deep frown. "I did not trick you. I only asked a simple question."

"Oh, right. A simple question that condemned me before I knew what was going on."

Ben continued calmly. "Your father wanted what he left you to be a remembrance of him alone, not something that got lost in the shuffle and forgotten. It seems to me that that's what an inheritance is about—something left behind to be remembered by—"

Molly cut him off. "I have no desire to remember my father at all," she said harshly.

Ben's frown grew even deeper. He placed his forearms on the table on either side of his plate and leaned slightly toward her. "And I think he was looking out for your future. I think he realized what kind of shape Mercer Moving and Storage was in and wanted to provide for you in the event that it went under. Better that than throwing good money after bad."

Molly's knuckles turned white as she gripped her glass of tea. Her voice was icy calm and sardonic, and her gaze could have frozen him. "I really should have known better. It's just like him to wave a carrot in front of my nose and then yank it out of reach when I need it most."

"Keeping your forty percent is in your best interests," Ben reasoned.

Molly took two deep breaths. She had been in business long enough to know that to lose her temper was to lose the battle. She tried another tack. "I haven't been able to pay Karen anything in profit sharing since before Christmas. As long as she was married, it didn't matter. Her husband supported the family. But now she and her kids have to have an income—in fact, Carl is holding money over her head like an ax. It is absolutely imperative that we sell out and rebuild Mercer Moving and Storage. *That* is what's in our best interests."

"I gave your father my solemn word. I have to honor that promise."

Better judgment or not, Molly lost her temper. "Forget a legacy from John Northrup," she mocked. "Believe me when I tell you that selling our inheritance from him now to save Mercer Moving and Storage is the single thing in his life he ever did that would benefit Karen and me. That is momentous enough to make it memorable. In fact, for him to come to our rescue at all should go down in the history books."

Ben watched her intently. "You know," he said kindly, "when you try to suppress what you're really feeling, it finds a way out, anyway." He reached across the table and covered her tightly clenched fist. "I don't think you're seeing this clearly. I think you're using it as an outlet—it feels better to be mad than to hurt like hell over your father's death."

Within the cocoon of his hand, her fist tightened. Molly drew in a deep breath, straightened her shoulders and gave a little laugh that sounded almost hysterical. "Now you're a psychiatrist, too?" she said with harsh sarcasm. "But not a very good one if you believe for one minute that I am not thinking straight because my *father* has just died."

It was unbelievably frustrating to see in his expression that that was just what he thought, regardless of anything she said. Molly wanted to hit him.

"Look," he said, "I can understand your position. But this is where I'm coming from—John Northrup was my friend and business partner. He taught me everything I know and he helped me get started. The clause in the partnership agreement that says no one but me can buy out his forty percent protected me at a time when he didn't have to agree to anything that protected me at his expense. When he knew he was dying, he asked for my word in return, and I intend to honor the promise I made. Understand that.''

She did understand. That was the irony of it. She remembered her father well enough to understand just how he could suck everyone in. Ben's sincerity cooled some of her anger. But inside, Molly was a volcano of rage, frustration and stress. She couldn't stay there and face him like a civil, rational businesswoman. She just couldn't.

''Then he's got us both trapped, and as always John Northrup gets his own way'' was all Molly said before she picked up her purse and left.

Chapter Five

"You're a lifesaver," declared Paula Brazos as she struggled to get out of Ben's car after their weekly Lamaze class the following afternoon.

Ben nodded his head in agreement. "True, but it's going to cost you."

"Name it."

"The recipe for those brownies you brought today. I barely got a bite—you pregos eat like weight lifters."

Having hoisted herself out, Paula bent over to peer back into the car, straining the width of the overalls she wore over a white tank top and ignoring the length of blond hair that fell over half her face. "No kidding," she said seriously. "Are you sure you don't mind watching Whitney for me tonight? Every babysitter I know is busy, and with having to take maternity leave any time now I just can't pass up overtime when it's offered."

Ben rolled his eyes. "I told you it was no big deal. She can play on my computer until I can get away. By the time we grab some dinner and an ice cream cone, it'll be time to bring her home. I'll still be able to get back to do closing."

Paula smiled at him. "You're a good guy, you know? I'm lucky to have you for a friend." Then her smile turned smug. "On the other hand, you're pretty lucky to have someone as swell as me give you my baking secrets—that recipe is on the back of the box of the store's brand of brownie mix. See you a little before five."

She closed the car door on Ben's laugh, and he watched until she was in the tiny house she rented for herself and her eight-year-old daughter.

They *were* just friends, he thought as he backed out of the driveway and headed for his Union Street restaurant. Strange how things were with people. Paula was a terrific-looking woman. Normally thin and lithe, she was the image of a California girl. She had a nice, even-tempered disposition, she was friendly, bright, had a good sense of humor, and he felt as comfortable with her as he did with his sisters. But that was it. No matter how hard he had tried to feel more than that for her, to convince himself that there was absolutely no reason in the world for him not to be attracted to her, he just wasn't.

On the other hand, five minutes after meeting Molly Mercer he had been hooked. There was no accounting for what drew people together and what didn't.

Thinking about Molly made him remember the past night. Just how mad at him was she, he wondered as he pulled into the parking lot at Boyd's. She had been up and gone from Churchill's before he could even get his napkin off his lap. He'd gone after her, but the manager had already been keeping an eye on them, suspicious of two people coming in and ordering everything on the menu. He had blocked the door and threatened to call the police if Ben didn't immediately pay the tab. By that time Molly had been long gone, and he had decided maybe it was better to let her calm down on her own rather than chance making matters worse by following her home.

"This is a fine kettle of fish you've gotten me into, John," he mumbled to himself as he locked his car and headed into the restaurant. "You could have at least left me a few clues about what's going on with your daughter."

There were a few late lunchers left amid the cleanup and preparations for the dinner crowd. Business was good—all three branches of Boyd's were thriving. So why was Molly against simply sitting back and enjoying the profits from her share? Maybe it wouldn't buy her company immediate redemption, but it wasn't small change, either, and it wasn't going to do her sister any harm.

Her sister.

Ben suddenly remembered Molly's argument about her sister needing the money to live. It made him feel guilty for his own hard line against buying them out. But had they gotten far enough into the discussion of what their share actually meant, Molly's sister might at least have been allowed a little peace of mind.

On impulse, he picked up the phone and dialed Molly's home number. When a woman who wasn't Molly answered, he guessed, "Karen?"

"Yes," she answered uncertainly.

"My name is Ben Boyd. Molly must have mentioned me to you, but I wanted to call and introduce myself."

The tone of the woman on the other end warmed slightly. "Yes, Molly told me about you."

"This probably seems odd to you. Please don't think Molly has blabbed about what's going on in your personal life, but she did tell me you're in need of an income Mercer Moving and Storage can't pay you. She left last night before I could get into it, and I just wanted you to know that profit sharing is figured quarterly. By the end of September or early October, you should have a check from your percentage."

"Oh," Karen said, the unexpectedness of this revelation obviously taking her aback. "I don't suppose you can tell me how much it will be?" Then she rushed in with an explanation before he could answer her. "It's just that I don't know whether to get a part-time job or a full-time one... Oh, well, I don't suppose it matters because I should get out of the house, anyway. Everyone says so, and I'm sure they're right. It's the only way a person can begin again, and I am going stir crazy..." She stopped as suddenly as she had started. "Lord, why am I telling you all this? I'm sorry, I'm not myself lately, and the longer I stay cooped up in these four walls, the battier I get."

Ben laughed kindly and gave her an easy out. "Cabin fever on the last day of August?"

"Cabin fever, yes. That's what it is. Sure."

Ben felt sorry for her. She sounded so confused and unsure and at odds. He wanted to help. "I don't know if you're interested, but I'm short a hostess here on Union in the afternoons. It would only take up a few hours of your time, but it would pay a little pocket money to tide you over. Then when you get your profit sharing, you can decide what you want to do from there."

"Oh, I wasn't asking for a job," Karen said in a hurry.

"I didn't think you were," he assured her quickly. "But would you like one, anyway?"

For a few moments she stumbled for something to say and then settled on, "I'm not really qualified for anything. Is it difficult?"

"No," he assured her. "You could come in tonight to learn the ropes and start tomorrow."

"It would get me out of the house," Karen mused more to herself than to him. "But I have to warn you, I'm not thinking too swiftly these days." Then she laughed, embarrassed. "I don't suppose that comes as news to you at this point."

"Actually, if you're thinking even half as fast as you're talking, you're in good shape," he said with amusement, and then coached, "First rule of getting a job—never do anything but talk yourself up. Now tell me you're absolutely sure you could do it, no problem at all. You're a whiz as a hostess."

Karen laughed and gamely repeated, "I'm absolutely sure I can do it, no problem at all. I'm a whiz as a hostess."

"Hired. Can you come in about four this afternoon? That way we can meet, and I can introduce you around before things get hectic."

"Oh, well," Karen hedged. "Sure. I suppose Molly will watch the girls for me."

"Great. Just come in the front door and ask for me. I'll tell the hostess to expect you."

"Thanks," she said as if she was suddenly unsure of what she had just agreed to.

Ben heard her hesitation and once more felt a wave of sympathy. "No pressure, Karen. I know you're going through a rough time right now. But it really is an easy job, and remember, you're not coming in as just any hostess, you're a part owner."

"That's right, I am, huh?" She sounded buoyed.

"See you at four?"

"I'll be there."

Ben hung up, his thoughts immediately turning to Molly again. "So you're going to pull baby-sitting duty tonight, too," he said to himself. Then he laughed. "Hot damn."

Nancy poked her head in the door to Molly's office. "You told me to let you know the minute the estimate for refinishing and replacing the antiques came in. Well, it's in. But I don't think you want to know what it is."

Molly looked up from her paperwork and grimaced at her friend and secretary. "If it's over a dollar fifty-nine, you're right, I don't want to know what it is."

Nancy's eyes widened to full moons. "Then you definitely don't want to know."

Molly motioned with a nod and pretended to be prepared to take her knocks. "Come on, let's get it over with. How bad can it be?"

Nancy closed the door after her and went to the desk, hesitantly handing her boss the paper. Molly glanced down at it, and all levity evaporated.

"That's the first time I've ever actually witnessed the color draining out of someone's face," her secretary said.

Molly's hands began to shake. The paper rattled then, so she put it down. "Seventeen *thousand* dollars?" she whispered in disbelief.

"Apparently the upwardly mobile Petrys had expensive taste in antiques."

"Guess so," was all Molly could manage to say as she rubbed her forehead with her fingertips. "Well." She took another look at the estimate. Her gaze was on the figures, but her eyebrows inched toward her hairline. "Think anyone else would be any cheaper?"

Nancy was solemn. "I made a dozen phone calls before I came in here. I read directly from that estimate so I'd know what to call the pieces and how to say what needed to be done. The bottom line is that that's as good as it gets."

Molly nodded. "I need to sleep on this," she said softly.

"Sure."

Easy agreement was a novelty from Nancy. It made Molly chuckle halfheartedly and look up at her friend. "What, no lecture? I must really be a sad case if you're foregoing even that."

Nancy shrugged. "You have enough on your shoulders right now. Besides, you already know I think you should opt out for Ben Boyd the hunk. It could be really romantic to work together side by side every day and on into the nights."

Now Molly laughed at her secretary's dreamy-eyed portrait of her partnership with Ben Boyd. "Forget I said anything and go back to giving me a break because I'm a sad case."

Nancy merely shrugged and left.

When the phone rang moments later, it was Molly who answered it. She was surprised and pleased to hear a somewhat happy lilt to her sister's voice, but that pleasure dimmed by the time Karen finished explaining her conversation with Ben.

"He really is a nice guy, Molly," her sister ended.

He's a buttinski, she thought, but didn't say it. "I think you're rushing things, Karen."

"What I'm doing is going crazy sitting around here alone all day."

"Why don't you come to the office, then?"

"Be honest, Molly. What would I do at Mercer Moving and Storage?"

"Filing, answering phones, helping Nancy."

"None of which needs to be done, does it?"

"Sure it does," Molly lied. Nancy was an extremely efficient person. But the thought of Karen working in Boyd's Restaurant rankled.

"Mercer Moving and Storage can't pay me," her sister reminded her.

Molly couldn't refute that. She also couldn't help feeling as if her sister was defecting to the enemy's camp where she would be working with Ben side by side every day and on into the nights....

Why in the world did Nancy's silly words repeat themselves in her thoughts?

Jealousy? That was ridiculous. Molly didn't have a jealous bone in her body. But what if Ben won Karen over to his side and she decided she didn't want to sell her share of his restaurants?

"Molly? Are you still there?" Karen said when a long silence had passed.

"Yes, I'm still here." But she couldn't remember what her sister had last said, so she couldn't respond to it.

"It's just kind of a lark, Molly," Karen went on without seeming to realize her sister's attention had drifted. "I need to get out, I can certainly use the money, and you know how crazy I am now. I don't think I can do any real damage seating people in a restaurant, but Lord knows the last thing you need around Mercer Moving and Storage is me screwing something up. You have enough problems without me adding to them." Then she repeated softly, "And there's the money."

There was no arguing that. Molly sighed resignedly. "Okay, you're right. Maybe with you on the inside, you can convince him to buy us out."

"Oh, I don't think so, Molly." Karen sounded scared. "I'm no good at any of that stuff. The business side is still yours."

"We have to work on your self-image. All you say lately is that you're no good at anything. What Carl did is an indication of something wrong with him, not you."

"Do you really think you can persuade Ben to change his mind and buy us out, after all?"

Molly noticed her sister's change of subject, but she let it slide. She knew that every time she spoke about her brother-in-law, her tone of voice gave her true feelings about him away. She also knew Karen was holding out hope and didn't want to hear it. "I don't know if I can get Ben to change his mind. I got mad and upset and did a dumb thing by running out like that when I should have held my ground and pushed for what we need. Now I'll just have to see what I can do from here."

"But you said last night that he seemed adamant," Karen reminded her.

"Yeah, well, I'm just as adamant."

"All the more reason that you better be the one to deal with it," Karen said with finality.

"Okay, don't worry about it."

"There's one other thing. Will you watch the kids for me tonight? The rest of the time I'll work while they're at school, but tonight I have to train."

"You know I will."

"Great. I'll get Amelia next door to watch them for the hour or so until you get home."

"I'll try to get out early," Molly said unenthusiastically.

"Thanks. I have to go and get ready. I'll see you when I get home tonight."

Molly hung up. "Damn you, Ben," she muttered to herself. Then she rolled her eyes at her own tone of voice. How could she damn him and have it come out sounding like an endearment?

But she knew how.

Molly placed the palms of her hands on her desk and pushed herself to her feet. With the march of the determined she headed out into the warehouse.

She couldn't let herself care about this guy. What she had to do, she told herself firmly, was to think about how to get him to buy back that forty percent so she could wipe him totally and completely out of her life.

Then she could box up that soft, vulnerable spot inside herself and put it away for good.

And when that was done, she'd be safe again.

* * *

"So here are the choices, guys," Molly said to her two nieces. "Wienies and beans or macaroni and cheese with hot dogs in it."

Eight-year-old Beth, who was a miniature replica of Karen, planted her elbows against her tiny waist, grabbed the hem of her T-shirt and stretched it up over her forearms as she pondered the matter of dinner. For Melissa there was no decision.

"Those are both hot dogs, and I hate 'em."

"I like hot dogs," Beth said in a tone that challenged her sister.

"Well, I don't," Melissa countered with a menacing stare. "And put your shirt down. I can see your belly button."

"So?"

"So," Molly jumped in, knowing all out war was on the way. "If you hate hot dogs, Lissa, what do you want for dinner?"

"T-bone steak," her niece said without missing a beat.

"Uh-huh. What's choice two?"

"I like shrimp," Melissa offered amiably enough.

"You know what I like to do sometimes?" Molly said as if it were a great treat.

"What?" the girls responded hopefully.

"Sometimes when I come home at night and it's hot like it is tonight and I don't feel like cooking and making the house even hotter, I fix myself a peanut butter and jelly sandwich and eat in the shade on the back porch. How's that sound?"

"I hate peanut butter," Beth announced, puckering her lips at the very thought.

"I don't like it, either," Melissa chimed in in a tone of voice that clearly said she thought her aunt was out of her mind.

Molly sighed exaggeratedly to let them know her patience was wearing thin. "Now, listen guys—"

Melissa laughed and interrupted. "You sound like my dad."

Before Molly had a comeback, the doorbell rang. As she headed toward the front of the house, she called back, "You two look in the pantry and the refrigerator and decide what we're going to eat. If you haven't made a decision by the time I get back, it's my choice and you'll just have to suffer. We'll eat peanut butter and jelly sandwiches."

"Not for dinner!" came the disapproving baritone from the other side of the open front door.

There was no mistaking that voice, or what it did to the surface of Molly's skin. Goose bumps the size of peas covered her flesh.

She rubbed both of her bare arms to get rid of the goose bumps as she stepped from the living room into the entranceway to find Ben standing at the screen.

He was dressed in dusty blue suit pants and a white dress shirt with the top button undone and the sleeves rolled to his elbows, and the bulk of his big, tall body filled the doorway as completely as it did Molly's senses. Even through the screen she could see the long creases that his smile formed in his cheeks. It was amazing how potent just the sight of him was.

"Ben..." She managed a very formal tone that didn't at all match the tight tank top and old faded jeans she wore.

"Molly..."

Then the worrier in Molly asserted itself. "Oh, my God, did something happen to Karen? Didn't she make it to work?"

Ben laughed. "Karen's fine. She made it to work. I left her seating a party of twelve like a pro."

Molly deflated slightly from the tension that had straightened her like a ramrod. "Then why are you here?" she blurted out before thinking about how it sounded.

"Do we have to talk through the screen?"

She hadn't thought about that, either. Molly unlatched the screen door and held it open for him, only then seeing the little girl playing with Beth's bike on the driveway. "Who's that?" she asked as he came in.

"Whitney belongs to an old friend. I'm baby-sitting tonight, and when Karen said you were, too, I thought we might as well join forces. We're on our way to Casa Bonita for dinner. I'd like it if you and your nieces would be my guests."

"Casa Bonita!" shrieked her own two charges from where they were spying behind Molly. Then Melissa announced, "We *love* to go there."

"I don't think—"

But Molly didn't have a chance to finish. Her nieces were begging in loud, discordant unison as Ben stood there smiling with clear satisfaction.

"It's okay with Karen. I checked before I came by," he offered.

"Yay! We can go! We can go!" the little girls chanted.

"And I already overheard that you were going to feed them peanut butter sandwiches for dinner. Shame on you," Ben put in over the commotion. Then he leaned very near, whispering in her ear, "You're out-numbered."

His breath was warm, he smelled faintly of after-shave, and all Molly could think was that she wished she had a bra on under her tank top.

She crossed her arms over her chest. "I brought some paperwork home and I just don't think—"

That was as far as she got a second time. Melissa and Beth's pleading raised two more octaves. It was Ben who finally got them to be quiet by talking in a voice so soft that they had to stop to hear him. "Why don't you girls go outside and meet Whitney—she's eight like Beth—and let me talk to your aunt?"

Until that moment neither of the girls had realized there was another guest. Melissa coerced her sister out the front door, and the last thing Molly heard was Beth hollering a warning. "Be careful, that's Speed Bike and you have to know how to handle him."

With her arms still protectively crossed over her chest, Molly heaved a sigh. "That was pretty slick."

Ben grinned. "Think of it this way. Everything has been so grim for them this week, they deserve a little entertainment."

"I was going to give them an impromptu picnic in the backyard."

"Can't compare to Casa Bonita. Besides—" he rested his forearm on her shoulder and pulled her ponytail off her neck "—Casa Bonita is air conditioned and you're not."

Two good points. The girls had had a grim week, and the thought of air conditioning was too wonderful to pass up. So was the thought of spending the evening with Ben, but she didn't want to admit that.

She stared up at him. "They eat like two horses. You're going to be sorry you did this."

He didn't look at all sorry. He looked delighted. "I'm willing to run the risk."

"I'll have to change."

Ben grabbed her arm before she had moved an inch. His gaze dropped for only a split second to her tank top, his grin very sensual, and he said, "Not on your life."

Molly had been feeling exposed before. Now she felt downright naked. She extracted her arm from his grip. "It'll only take a minute."

"Party pooper," he called after her as she climbed the stairs to her bedroom.

"Whatever you do, don't say that word," Molly chastised.

"Party?"

"No. Poop. It's Melissa and Beth's favorite word. Get them started and they'll be finding a way to get it into the conversation all night."

"Duly warned. I'm going to get them all into the car," Ben hollered.

"Okay. I'll be right there."

Molly took a shirt out of her closet, draped it on the bed beside her bra, grasped the bottom of her tank top and barely began to pull it up when her body came alive. Her nipples hardened, and a tingling sensation tantalized that spot between her legs.

She'd gone absolutely nuts. A few minutes ago she had been wishing for armor—or at least for a bra. Now the bra waited on the bed, and so did the armor in the form of a high necked big shirt. Suddenly she didn't want to be swathed in yellow cotton. She wanted to stay feeling sexy in the tank top.

Nuts. Absolutely.

She heard the horn honk outside, followed by Ben hollering up, "That was the kids. Take your time."

If she went out in this tank top when she had already made such a big deal out of wanting to change it, he'd know. She swallowed hard.

"Decide, Molly, decide," she ordered herself. She should wear the armor even though she didn't want to.

The horn honked again, and once more she heard Ben's voice through her open window. "That was your niece. The natives are getting restless."

Molly let out a tight little shriek.

Then she left the bra on the bed, grabbed up the shirt and slipped it on, leaving it untucked and unbuttoned. The tank top still peeked through. Then she went out to join the man who aroused feelings in her she didn't know she was capable of.

In the same way the meal at a dinner theater is not by any means the main attraction, the food at Casa Bonita was far less important than the atmosphere.

Behind an ornate fountain, Casa Bonita's facade was a pink stucco structure like an elaborate Spanish church beneath a high bell tower. To step inside was to leave Denver and enter a Mexican village.

After they had wound through what looked like streets and courtyards to order and then get trays of unexceptional food, tables were available in mining caves, around a small pool, in gazebos, in areas that looked like Mexican cantinas, even in a theater where magicians or jugglers entertained from the red velvet curtained stage.

Ben, Molly and the girls were seated in the caverns—the quietest section in the place. What that

meant was that Melissa, Beth and even the more subdued Whitney were less interested in food than in getting into the thick of things.

Throughout the meal Molly marveled at Ben's handling of the fidgety children. He invented games and
teased them into peals of giggles and challenges that
made them eat even when their appetites had disappeared in the excitement of their surroundings. She
admired and appreciated his good-natured patience
when her own was stretched to the limits.

"Eat your dinner, too, Ms. Mercer," he said with a
mischievous sparkle in his steel-gray eyes. "You
missed the meal last night. I'd hate to see it happen
again."

Molly flinched at the thought of the past evening,
having forgotten she had intended to apologize. "Last
night was different," she said feebly, watching her
fork as she toyed with her Spanish rice.

"Yeah, you were mad at me," he teased.

"I wasn't exactly mad at you."

"Funny, you seemed mad."

"I was mad at circumstances, maybe, but not at
you."

He ran his fingers up the side of her neck, inside her
shirt collar and ended tugging playfully on her earlobe. "I'm glad to hear it."

"I'm not giving up, though," she warned him.

Ben only smiled. "I didn't think you would. But this
is not the time or place. That's why I picked it."

"Underhanded, was it?" she said, amazing herself
with the coquetry in her own voice.

"Absolutely."

By then the three girls had been put off all they
could be and there was no more holding them down.

And since Molly's skin was beginning to erupt into those gargantuan goose bumps again, she seized the distraction. "The natives are restless."

For a long moment his gaze stayed on her, devouring her, and then he spoke to the table at large. "Okay, gang, let's go."

Casa Bonita was like a Mexican village at fiesta time. They watched all the shows in the theater, had the girls' pictures taken in the jail, listened to the roving guitarists and watched the flamenco dancers.

In the piñata-festooned marketplace they had Ben's caricature done, bought cotton candy, watched a puppet show, squeezed through the pirate cave tunnel and had Molly's fortune told. Just when Ben and Molly had had enough, they found the game room—complete with video games, pinball and ski ball.

By that time all three little girls knew exactly how to work Ben to get what they wanted. Rather than leave as they had planned, he supplied them with quarters, explained where he and Molly would be, left Melissa in charge and then led Molly to a quiet table back in the caverns for iced tea.

"You're amazing, Boyd," she said when she had settled into the booth with a sigh.

"Amazingly wonderful, handsome, brilliant and sexy?" he teased over his own tea, referring to her fortune that said she would have a wonderful, handsome, brilliant man in her future.

"Amazing with kids. And the fortune didn't say anything about sexy."

"I just threw that in."

"It seems strange for a man who's never been married to have such an easy rapport with kids."

He shrugged. "I have seven nieces and nephews. And I like kids."

"So you volunteer to baby-sit for your friends, too?"

"I didn't volunteer. I was asked. What about you? You may not know better than to force-feed them peanut butter for dinner, but you seem to like your nieces."

"I do. They're good kids. I won't mind if they end up living with me."

"As in their parents divorcing?"

Molly nodded.

Ben sobered. "Is it going that far?"

"It's hard to tell. If it were I...but it isn't. It's Karen's decision, and I'm trying to keep my mouth shut. She did mention something about everyone making mistakes last night, so she may be weakening."

"And you don't approve. Why do I have the feeling you don't have much respect for the institution of marriage?"

"I don't know, why do you?" Molly answered evasively.

"You like kids, you're thirty-three years old." His eyes devoured her appreciatively. "You're terrific looking and intelligent. How come you've never been married?"

Molly laughed. "How come you got to be brilliant and I only got to be intelligent?"

"Okay, brilliant. Answer my question."

"I almost did once. I was twenty. The invitations were sent, everything was set to go. I came close to being left standing at the altar."

"The guy was congenitally stupid."

"The guy was like most guys—congenitally commitmentphobic."

"Commitmentphobic?"

"Scared to death of keeping a commitment."

Ben studied her for a long moment, his eyes piercing. Then he breathed out a sad little laugh and frowned at her. "You say that without bitterness, as if it's universally applicable."

"I did, didn't I?" Molly agreed a little smugly, as if she knew something he didn't. But before anything more could be said, the three little girls reappeared.

"Tapped out, huh, kids?" Ben asked, then looked at his watch. "Just in time, too. We need to get Whitney back home."

"It's past Melissa and Beth's bedtime, too," Molly confirmed above the chorus of moans and groans.

Ben slid out of the booth to put Melissa in a headlock, ruffle Whitney's hair and then grab Beth around the scruff of the neck. "Come on, don't tell me you three haven't had enough."

Molly watched as her two nieces responded to the roughly tender affection with giggles and obvious pleasure, beaming beneath his flattering teasing. She wondered if Ben knew how much Beth and Melissa had needed not only this evening but this kind of attention from a man when they were missing their own father so much? Did he know that such small things could remind them that they were special?

But whether he knew it or not, she did. She understood it all too well. At least she and Karen had had their grandfather and their uncles. Beth and Melissa wouldn't even have that. Suddenly Molly's heart felt swollen.

Then Ben reached out a hand to her. "Come on, Mercer, let's get these giggle boxes out of here."

Molly didn't want to look up at him, afraid he would see how much his kindness had moved her. But she took his hand. It was odd that it suddenly felt different to her, that for some reason her own hand in his seemed to fit, and more, to belong. It was unnerving, so as soon as she was on her feet, she let go and plunged her hands into the pockets of her jeans.

"They might stop giggling if you stopped tickling them," she observed wryly to hide her own emotions.

"What fun would that be?" he asked as he continued his attack all the way to the cashier and then out to the car.

He had them singing "Row Row Row Your Boat" all the way to Whitney's house. Once there, he left Melissa and Beth seeing who could hold her breath the longest while he walked the other little girl to the door. Molly was grateful for the silence, watching him as he went.

Through the screen door Molly saw Whitney's mother approach. She was very young. The attractive blonde smiled at Ben in a way that seemed intimate. She wore a loose caftan that covered a body Molly imagined to be as lovely as it was long.

Whitney walked into the house between the two adults, leaving them alone in the doorway. They chatted for a few minutes, then Ben leaned down slightly, the woman raised up on tiptoe, they kissed, and he was on his way back to the car.

"Paula asked us all in, but I turned her down," he said as he got behind the wheel again. "You did want to get these other two urchins home, didn't you?"

There had been such familiarity in that kiss that Molly felt suddenly very uncomfortable. "Yes, I did," she answered somewhat stiltedly. "But it was nice of her to offer. Have you known Whitney's parents long?" She was fishing, but she couldn't help it.

"I've never met her father. He and Paula were divorced by the time we met."

"I see," Molly said. Suddenly she saw more than she wanted to.

Ben started the car, glancing over at her as he did. "That sounded icy."

"I just assumed . . ."

"That the friend I was sitting for was either male or a couple," Ben finished, unperturbed.

"Something like that."

"Paula's a single parent. Things aren't easy for her, and I help out when I can. I'm going to be her Lamaze coach."

It came out so easily. "Her Lamaze coach," Molly repeated. "She's pregnant?"

"You couldn't tell? No, I don't suppose you could in that thing she was wearing. Actually she's due any time."

Beth and Melissa had fallen asleep in the back seat, and the silence was suddenly tense. *You're a dummy, Mercer,* Molly thought to herself.

Ben took his eyes off the road for a moment and looked over at her. She could feel his gaze, but remained staring straight ahead, wishing her nieces were still making their usual racket.

He reached across and squeezed the back of her neck, much as he had Beth's before. "What are you thinking, lady?" he asked in his deep baritone voice.

"Nothing."

"It's been my experience that every time a woman says nothing she means the opposite."

"You ought to know."

"Meaning?"

"Apparently you've had enough experience."

She heard him chuckle. It was the most irritating sound Molly had ever endured.

"You're jealous," he taunted delightedly.

"You're crazy."

"I like it."

"You're crazy."

"I'm going to bask in it for a minute before I tell you the truth."

While he did just that Molly stewed. Jealous? Her? He really was crazy if he thought she cared what he did or with whom. She cared about Mercer Moving and Storage, about her sister and her nieces, about his buying her out of his restaurants and getting totally and completely out of her life forever.

Ben cleared his throat. "I'm Paula's Lamaze coach because we've been friends for a long time. The father of her baby deserted her, and she needed me to stand in. She's like one of my sisters."

Sure. "I don't care."

"Keep that tone up and I'm going to have to turn on the heater."

Molly pulled her shirt more tightly around herself.

"You're going to love my brother when you meet him," Ben said, still unperturbed. "He's as suspicious as you are."

"You can pull into the driveway."

He did. When he had turned the ignition off, he pivoted on the seat to face her, reaching over to grasp the nape of her neck again, turning her head to look into her eyes. He was very serious now. And very blunt. "I got close to Paula about a year and a half ago. We were friends, both lonely, and at the time it seemed like a good idea to let it go further. It was definitely not a good idea. We didn't hit it off. Didn't mesh. There was nothing there. So we went back to being friends. That's it. Nothing at all like what I feel for you."

What did he feel for her? It was on the tip of Molly's tongue to ask, but pride wouldn't let her. "It doesn't matter."

"It matters to me. I care for you. More every time I'm with you. I haven't been involved with anyone at all in nearly a year. I've never had anyone do to me what you do to me. You're right, I am crazy. Crazy about you. I want you in my life—and I'm not talking about business." Somehow his hand had slipped from the back of her neck to cup her chin. He had moved near. He was staring into her eyes, his own shadowed by a solemn frown. And then his mouth lowered to hers, at first lightly, but it rapidly grew harder, more urgent.

His arms went around her, pulling her up close to his broad chest. His lips parted, his tongue thrust into her mouth, finding hers, circling it.

She had been jealous, she admitted to herself now. Watching him kiss—however platonically—his friend had made her crazy and left her with a sudden drive to stake a claim on him. She didn't want anyone else to have a right to him, to wanting him, to being with him.

His mouth instantly reignited the sensual feelings that had kept her braless and dressed in the tank top, only now they were sharper, more intense. Now they were made stronger by a need she had never known.

She clasped his neck between her hands, feeling the strength in the cords and tendons straining there. She let her lips slacken more and then open wide, meeting and matching his, dancing now with her tongue around his, learning the contours of his mouth in the same way he had learned hers.

His hands slid inside her shirt and down her bare arms, trailing electrical currents. Then he hooked his fingers in the shoulder strap of her tank top and followed the curve downward until the backs of his fingers were against the sides of her breasts.

Molly felt her nipples harden against the tight tank top just before he slipped one hand under the T-shirt and covered her breast fully with his palm, pressing, kneading gently. Amazing explosions of desire burst in her. It felt so good that she could hardly breathe.

And then, from the back seat Melissa moaned in her sleep, and Molly jumped half a foot and severed their kiss. She had forgotten her nieces only a few feet away. They both had.

"No," she whispered, horrified, trying to catch her breath, to convince her body she shouldn't be doing this. She rested her forehead against Ben's collarbone.

But rather than take it too seriously, he chuckled, a deep, almost soundless rumble beneath her forehead. "They're dead to the world back there," he assured her so softly that his voice was little more than a hot burst of air against the top of her head. He took her face in both of his hands and raised it to his. "There's no harm done, Molly."

"I have to get them inside," she said in a hurry, afraid of the strength and extent of her own emotions.

For a moment he held her face, staring into her eyes, then he kissed her once more, a slow, lazy, lingering kiss, before releasing her.

Molly got out of the car as if it were on fire—as surely her senses were. Just then Karen drove up and offered her the excuse she needed to end this evening.

The three of them got Melissa and Beth out of the car. From there only Molly and Karen herded them into the house, thanking Ben and insisting he go back to work. Only after she was safely inside did Molly hazard a look outside. There he was, leaning against the front fender of his car, his legs stretched out, crossed at the ankles, his arms folded over his chest. He was watching her retreat, somehow conveying that he knew it for what it was, that he was allowing it this time.

And the only thing Molly really wanted was to go back out to him, to his arms, to his mouth, to the feelings that were still alive, unsatiated.

Of course she didn't do that.

Instead she locked the front door and turned out the porch light. But she realized that somehow in those few simple moments when he had shown her nieces such simple affection, what had been a physical attraction had turned into something more, something softer, warmer, deeper. Something ultimately more powerful.

Chapter Six

The doorbell was chiming in rapid, persistent bursts when Molly turned off the shower the following morning. She hurriedly wrapped a towel around her wet hair and pulled on her terry cloth robe.

"Karen, Karen, Karen," she said to herself as she did, shaking her head. "Are you going to make it through this, kiddo?"

Yesterday her sister had left to take the girls to school and forgotten her keys. The day before, Karen's car wouldn't start in the school parking lot and she had had to go into the school in her nightgown to call Molly, only to have the janitor come in in the middle of the conversation to tell her he had gotten it started without any problem. The day before that Karen hadn't been able to work the dead bolt on the front door to let herself back in the house.

So what was it today? Molly wondered as she descended the stairs. It must be the worst yet because the doorbell was being pounded.

"It's okay, I'm right here," Molly called through the solid oak panel. "Just give me a minute."

But it wasn't Karen standing on the front porch when Molly opened the door. It was Carl Dune. She stiffened.

"I've been ringing this damn bell for ten minutes," he said, his tone as angry as his expression.

Molly answered him as coldly as dry ice. "I was in the shower. I didn't hear anything until I turned the water off."

"Where's Karen?" he demanded.

"Not here." She gripped the edge of the front door and dropped her glance to the screen door handle to see if it was locked. It wasn't. She wanted to reach down and lock it, but refrained.

"Where the hell is she?" Carl ground out through clenched teeth.

"You have a lot of nerve, do you know that? What right do you have to come here being nasty and demanding? *You* caused this and *you* agreed to give her time out."

"Don't push me, Molly. My life is falling down around my ears. My job is in jeopardy because the woman I don't want won't leave me alone. And instead of Karen moving home where she belongs so we can put this behind us, I find out this morning from a so-called friend that my wife is out working nights in some damn restaurant."

"Play the game, pay the price."

"I want to talk to her."

"She isn't here," Molly repeated, glad that it was the truth.

No sooner had she thought it than the white station wagon pulled up in front of the house.

"Keep in mind," she said to her brother-in-law as he turned to glare at Karen coming up the walk. "That *you* are in the wrong, Carl."

"Butt out, Molly."

For a fleeting moment Molly considered opening the screen door into the back of his head, but again she refrained. She wasn't pleased to see Karen smile feebly at the man as she climbed the porch steps. In fact it rankled more than Carl's attitude. She would have preferred her sister greet him with all the disgust he deserved.

Abruptly, she turned and went back upstairs to dress. At first the only sounds that drifted up to her were those of normal speaking voices. But by the time she had curled her hair, applied a light dusting of blush to her cheekbones and was ready to put her clothes on, Karen's and Carl's shouts were echoing through the house.

The sound made Molly's heartbeat speed up and the muscles in her neck tighten. She was suddenly a child again, listening to her parents fight in their bedroom. Her stomach lurched, and her upper lip began to perspire. She was afraid. So afraid. Her mother was crying. She could tell. That sound scared her even more than the angry voices, because her mother never cried unless something was really wrong.

Then a particularly strident epithet from Carl Dune penetrated Molly's flashback.

It wasn't her mother crying. It was Karen.

But her own dilemma was the same—should she go to Karen, interfere? Or stay in her room, pretend she didn't know what was going on?

A hard knot formed in the pit of Molly's stomach. She wanted to go downstairs and protect her sister, throw her brother-in-law out on his ear, call the police and have him arrested for trespassing or disturbing the peace or anything that would see him as humiliated as his affair had left Karen.

But it wasn't her place.

Then the slam of the front door spared her the decision, leaving Molly with a well-remembered feeling of impotence.

The house was quiet except for the soft sound of her sister crying downstairs.

"Bastard," Molly whispered. Quickly, she finished tucking her shirt into her slacks, slipped on her shoes and went to Karen.

Her sister was sitting like a rag doll on the couch, her face once again a red, puffy mass of misery. "Now he says if I don't come home he's going to sue me for custody of the girls."

Molly slapped lint from her black slacks so hard that it hurt. "On what grounds? He agreed to your moving out—it wasn't desertion. Then you took a job to support them when he refused to."

When Karen cried harder Molly consciously spoke in a softer tone of voice. "I'm sorry. I just don't want to see you browbeaten by him."

"I know. And you're right. But I still feel so awful."

Molly went into the kitchen and came back with the tissue box, hating what she was about to say, but remembering that hopeful smile on her sister's face as she had approached her husband half an hour ago. "Would it be any better if you went back there and hashed it all out between the two of you, saw a counselor or something? The girls could stay with me."

Karen blew her nose. "Thank goodness the girls weren't here to hear this round, huh? I remember how awful that was...."

Molly didn't say anything to that. "I'll support whatever you want, kiddo, you know that."

"I don't want to go back, not like this, not when I'd feel as if it wasn't my choice. But maybe Carl and I should see a counselor. We're certainly not getting anywhere this way." Then Karen looked at the wooden Ben Franklin clock over the fireplace. "You're going to be late for work again this morning. Good thing no one can fire you."

"I do need to get going," Molly admitted, picking up her purse. As she took out her car keys, she suggested, "Maybe today isn't the best day to start your new job."

"No, I want to go. It's better than staying here and thinking about all this."

"It's up to you. I'll call you in a couple of hours to check on things."

Karen walked with Molly to the door, trying on a smile that didn't fit. "And just last week you had a nice, quiet, peaceful, well-ordered life," she said to her sister.

Molly laughed ruefully. "So did you. I'll talk to you later. If you need me in the meantime, you know where I am."

"Sure. Don't worry about me."

Molly hesitated for a minute and then gave her sister a hug. Whether Karen needed that reassuring contact or not, Molly did.

As she got into her car, she realized how difficult it was to shake the feelings that had come to life as she overheard Karen and Carl's argument, and for some reason those same feelings made her think about Ben.

Fantasy was a dangerous thing, she thought as she merged onto the highway. It lulled a person into forgetting the realities.

When she was twenty, she had believed in the fantasy of love. She had believed Dave was special, that he really did love her as he said he did, that they would get married and live happily ever after—forever. Obviously that had been a fantasy. The same fantasy her mother had had. The same fantasy Karen had had.

This week, even in the midst of her sister's personal trauma, Molly had taken the first few nebulous steps into that fantasy again—in the form of Ben Boyd. She realized now she had denied the reality that love never lasted.

What she felt for Ben was powerful and getting more powerful by the minute. That was why she *had* to get out of it. So the first thing she did when she got to Mercer Moving and Storage was close her office door, sit behind her desk and dial Ben's phone number. When he answered, her tone was clipped and totally businesslike.

"I want to arrange a meeting with you to discuss this partnership," she told him bluntly.

"Molly?"

But she cut him off. "I shouldn't have rushed out of Churchill's the other night without talking more about it. I let my temper get the better of me and now I want to rectify that."

"You know," Ben said, sounding confused, "I haven't been up very long, so maybe I've missed something. Is this Molly Mercer, the same lady I left eleven hours ago after a terrific evening and a good-night kiss that could have put a man with a weaker heart into cardiac arrest?"

Molly didn't like the warmth that reminder sent through her. "You know this is me," she said inanely, not knowing what else to say, her tone of voice hostile.

"Is this a joke?"

"Of course not."

"Did you remember something I said after I left that made you mad?"

"No."

"Did someone call you up in the middle of the night and slander my good name?"

"No."

"Then what the hell is going on? If I may ask."

"Last night was just..." She didn't know how to finish it. Wonderful was the only adjective that came to mind, but she couldn't lose herself to him. "Last night was just for the kids' sake."

Ben laughed at that. "What benefit was there for them in that kiss?" When she didn't answer, he went on. "I think I'm beginning to understand you, but let's see if I have it straight. If we have a rotten time—like at Churchill's—you feel safe and secure. So following that up by seeing me is not an ominous proposition. But have a night like last night where we enjoy ourselves and end it...the way we did...and for some reason it scares you. So you swing a hundred and eighty degrees in the other direction and want to freeze me out. Am I close?''

Right on target actually, but he didn't need to know that. "I don't want this in my life right now."

"Or ever, if I'm any judge," he said, undaunted. "But it's here, regardless."

Molly tried to guide him back to the course she had set. "About the meeting."

Ben ignored the attempt. "Know anything about fight or flight? I don't know why, but you seem to see me as some kind of danger. Let's talk about it."

"I want to see you about this partnership. That's it. Take my word for it."

"No."

"No? What do you mean no?"

"No, I won't take your word for it. Yes, I'd love to see you, in fact I was going to call you in a couple of hours to set that up myself. The partnership needs to be discussed—as far as how it works, what you'll get out of it. If it makes you feel better to call seeing me a business meeting, I'm game. Call it a business meeting."

"Fine. When?" she clipped out. Let him think anything he wanted. She knew what she was doing.

"Tonight, seven. I'll pick you up for dinner."

"I'm working late tonight."

"On a Friday night before a holiday weekend?"

"It's been a bad week. I didn't get everything I needed to done, and Karen has a friend coming over to the house so I'm going to use the time to my advantage."

"Have it your way, then. I'll get my manager to do closing and pick you up for a late dinner."

"I'm working *very* late. I was hoping you could come to my office sometime today." She wanted it on her own territory, in her office where business felt like business.

"Wooo, I must really have gotten under your skin last night," he said with a confident chuckle.

"Like poison ivy," she answered facetiously, knowing it was uncalled for. She took a deep breath, held it for a moment and then sighed. She was going to apologize for the comment, but what came out was a plea that revealed too much. "Please don't push this, Ben. I know what I want. More important, I know what I *don't* want—I don't want romance, involvement, any of what's happening here."

"Why not?" he asked gently, rationally.

"I just don't."

"Okay," he agreed amiably.

Sudden panic struck, and Molly had the urge to recall everything she had said.

Then Ben went on. "No romance or involvement. How about straight sex between friends?"

It took her by surprise, unarmed her and very nearly made her laugh. She was in deep, deep trouble with this man and Molly knew it. "I'm serious, Ben," she tried to reaffirm.

"Too serious. Or at least you're trying to force yourself to be even when deep down there's some frivolous things happening."

Frivolous? Hardly frivolous. Tumultuous, maybe. "The business meeting, remember?" She sounded in control again.

He sighed, but somehow she knew he wasn't conceding. "Name the time and I'll be there."

"Since I'm on home ground, whatever's best for you."

"I'll be there at eight tonight. Don't eat, I'll bring a basket and we'll have a warehouse picnic. No romance in that."

"Business," she reiterated.

"Food is my business. Yours, too, partially."

Molly sighed. She had to get Ben out of her life so she could be safe again, and if it meant having dinner with him one more time, then she'd just have to do it. "All right. Eight," she agreed tersely.

"Molly?"

"I'm here."

His voice was suddenly as low as if someone were listening and this was for her ears alone. "I really am wild about you."

Molly's only answer was another sigh before she hung up.

All the warehouse doors were locked when Ben knocked at a little before eight that night, so Molly had to walk from her office and past Nancy's desk to let him in. The evenly paced clips of her small heels on the concrete floor sounded confident, and that reassured her. She could handle this. She could keep this on a purely business level. She could convince him to buy her out and disappear from her life as if they'd never met.

"Is that you, Ben?" she called before unlocking the door just for precaution's sake. Her own voice came out forcefully, further buoying her.

"It's me," he called back.

The deep timbre of his voice struck a chord inside her, but she told herself she could ignore it.

Molly opened the door and there he stood with a picnic basket in one hand, a bottle of wine in the other, and the warmest smile on a face that could have been on the cover of a magazine.

All of a sudden the high collar of her blouse seemed too tight and constricting. Molly stepped back so he could come in, but rather than just passing her by, he stopped directly in front of her, grinned down into her face for a moment and then kissed her as if he had the right.

Molly was instantly asizzle, the memory of the kiss that had ended the previous night flaming to life in her mind.

"I'd tell you how good it is to see you, but I can't put it into words," he said in that same intimate tone of voice he had used on the telephone that morning.

Molly didn't respond. She merely closed the warehouse door and locked it before leading the way back to her office.

"I appreciate your coming here. I imagine Friday is a big night for you," she said as she sat behind her desk, stiff and straight.

"It is." He set the picnic basket on her desktop.

"I'm really not hungry. Could we just get down to business?"

"Sure. We'll start with wine."

"Ben..."

"Molly..." he mimicked, uncorking the bottle. "We'll just let this breathe for a few minutes."

Good idea. She wished she could, but every breath brought her the clean, intoxicating scent of him and insidiously eroded her resolve. She closed her eyes and dropped her head. "Why can't you make this easy for me?" she said to herself.

Before she realized it, he had rounded the desk and was massaging her neck. "I'm trying to make everything as easy for you as I can. It's you that's fighting things."

His big hands circled the outside of her collar, his thumbs reaching up into her hair to press into her nape. It felt good. Too good.

She straightened. "It's imperative that you buy Karen and me out of your restaurants and that you and I don't see any more of each other," she blurted out.

Ignoring the abrupt movement, Ben now massaged her shoulders, digging his thumbs into the tense muscles of her back. "It wouldn't make any difference if we did dissolve our business partnership. I'd still be after you, Molly," he told her very seriously. "I want you."

He hit a particularly sensitive muscle, and Molly rolled involuntarily into it. "No, no, no," she said not nearly as forcefully as she intended.

"Yes, yes, yes," he countered with amusement in his voice. "We're right together."

Before she could argue the point, the phone rang, sounding odd and out of place in the intimate quite.

Even so, Molly was grateful for the interruption. She shrugged out of Ben's reach and picked it up, ignoring the kiss he pressed to her earlobe before beginning to unload the basket.

"Mercer Moving and Storage."

As Molly listened to the impersonal voice on the other end, her grip on the phone tightened. The tension returned to her neck and shoulders threefold, and the sensual feelings she had been unsuccessfully fighting before were thoroughly tamped down by a rush of adrenaline.

When she had all the information she needed, she hung up and grabbed her purse as if nothing had been going on only moments earlier. "One of my trucks skidded off a road and overturned down an embankment behind the brewery. I have to get out there."

The serious tone of Molly's side of the conversation had already sobered Ben. "Was anyone hurt?"

"Yes, my driver, but they wouldn't tell me how badly."

"Come on, I'll take you."

Molly didn't argue. Her mind was spinning a mile a minute with worries—and though it was not comfortable, it was somehow preferable to thinking about the feelings she had for Ben.

Flashing red and blue lights illuminated the sight of the accident as Ben and Molly arrived at the scene after a tense, silent twenty-minute drive. There were four police cars, two fire engines, three security trucks from the brewery, an ambulance and the usual assortment of curious onlookers.

Ben had barely stopped the car before Molly bounded out of it. Her first concern was for the driver. But there was no one to ask as police, firemen, security guards and paramedics all worked to free him from the cab.

One glance down the embankment was enough to tell Molly the truck was totaled. From the look of the trailer, it had rolled at least once and landed nose down, taking a full side of fence with it, but stopping just short of hitting the brewery itself.

For a split second the sight of it made her want to sit down and cry. She had never dealt with anything like this before, and she didn't know where to begin now. Rather than thinking about it, her mind kept rehashing things that no longer mattered. This had been an easy apartment move with the client paying extra to have the job done this evening. But maybe she shouldn't have taken the work. Maybe if it hadn't been dark. Maybe Dick, the driver, had been too tired for the overtime. Maybe he had been in a hurry...

"Oh, God, what if it was a mechanical failure?" she said, not even realizing she had spoken aloud or that Ben was at her side to hear.

He took her arm to steady her as she watched the police and paramedics lifting the driver up the embankment on a stretcher. "It's not likely, Molly," he said into her ear, his voice as comforting and supporting as his hand on her arm. "Don't borrow trouble."

Molly introduced herself to the first state patrolman to climb up the embankment, but before he had a chance to answer her questions, the stretcher bearers reached the top, too, and Dick, the driver, caught sight of her. His left arm was in a sling on top of the sheet that covered him from shoulders down, and one side of his face was bloody, but he managed to lift his head off the stretcher.

"This is your fault!" he shouted weakly. "Rotten outfit sticking me with an old heap of a truck. You'll pay for this."

All eyes turned to Molly. She felt as though she was going to faint. She started to apologize, but Ben must have guessed her intention and stopped her.

"Don't say anything. You don't know if he's right, and until you do, you don't want to say anything that could be construed as an admission."

Ben's advice was good, but it didn't help the guilt she felt. What if it *wasn't* the driver's fault. Her stomach felt queasy, and the pungent smell of yeast and hops coming from the brewery didn't help. She reeled slightly. Ben's grip on her arm tightened, and he pulled her in close to his side.

Helplessly, she watched as the stretcher was loaded into the ambulance. Then a police officer with a clipboard came up to verify that she was responsible for the vehicle sitting like a crashed dive bomber only a few yards from the brewery.

Ben leaned toward her ear. "I'll be right back." Then he squeezed her arm reassuringly and headed toward the ambulance.

Molly answered the questions the officer asked, her eyes on Ben the whole time. Yes, she was covered by insurance. The truck was over twelve years old, but her mechanic had orders to check every truck out from top to bottom once a month. No, she didn't know much about the driver. He was new and from out of state. She hadn't checked his driving record, had only taken his word for the fact that he'd never had an accident. He had been vouched for by one of her other drivers, a long-time, trusted employee.

When the ambulance finally drove off, it was at a normal speed without the lights flashing. Molly was as glad to see that as she was to have Ben back at her side. This time he put his arm around her and pulled her in close to his body. The simple, comforting gesture was like a tonic to her, strengthening her in some indefinable way.

The officer excused himself to answer a call on his radio, and in the few moments they were alone, Ben said, "I talked to the paramedic. He couldn't guarantee it, but he said it looked to him like your driver got away with a broken arm and a few cuts that might need stitches, but that's about all. He'll be fine."

"Thank God," Molly murmured. "Now let's just hope the problem wasn't with the truck so he doesn't have grounds to sue."

Ben's arm around her tightened as he shook his head and smiled down at her. "You really are a worrier, aren't you?"

But Molly was too distracted by those worries to answer him.

By the time decisions needed to be made about getting the truck out, it was Ben and the police who made them and then oversaw the operation that took two tow trucks to haul the wreckage up the embankment.

Molly spent most of that time in the back seat of a state patrol car filling out papers. Several times she looked up from what she was doing to find Ben dealing with the police or the tower. Each time she just sat and watched for a while. Sharing a burden was a novelty to her. A nice novelty.

By the time everything was wrapped up, it was nearly midnight. Molly collapsed into the passenger seat of Ben's car, let her head fall back and closed her eyes. "I think I want to be in another time and place."

Ben draped his arm across the top of the seat and squeezed the back of her neck. "Detroit, 1896?"

Molly laughed softly and opened one eye to stare at him. "What?"

"Another time and place. How about San Francisco, 1920? Or New York at the turn of the century?

Or were you thinking future? Saturn, 2022? Or . . . my place for a modest dish of scrambled eggs? It'll take about fifteen minutes to get there.''

In the back of her mind a feeble voice told her not to do this, but it was so feeble that she ignored it. Molly was weary. There were lots of other words for it—worried, strained, stressed, overwhelmed—but at that moment it was just plain weariness. And there beside her was Ben, yet again a shelter from the storm. Her car was at the warehouse, but the warehouse seemed so far away, so cold and ugly and fraught with all the things she didn't want to think about any more tonight. There was home, but home meant Karen and the girls and their problems and Molly's own old, ugly memories.

And there was Ben's apartment.

No matter how much she wished it wasn't true, what that meant to her was Ben and warmth and solace and comfort and freedom from all the rest. And if it also meant indulging in those other feelings that she undeniably had for him—those feminine, sensual, uninhibited feelings—well, suddenly she didn't care.

Tomorrow could take care of itself. For the next hour Molly was going to let Ben take care of her.

"No monkeying around?" she asked because it soothed her conscience.

Ben smiled over at her. "If that's how you want it."

Was it? Even Molly didn't know. That, she decided, could take care of itself, too. "Okay, I guess I can pick up my car tomorrow," she agreed. Then she closed her eyes again, rested her head back against the seat and didn't think another thing throughout the fifteen-minute drive, letting the hum of the engine and the soft drone of classical music lull her.

Ben's apartment was in a three-block cluster of brown buildings off Union Street. As if he knew she needed a little withdrawal, he didn't say anything until he had gotten out of the car, opened her door for her and guided her up the two flights of stairs to his third-floor apartment. When he did speak again, his tone was light and easy, as if they both hadn't just spent a tension-filled few hours. "You're in luck—my cleaning lady came this morning."

Molly wrinkled her nose. "Is it awful otherwise?"

"My brother, Rick, thinks it should be condemned," he said as he unlocked the door and pushed it open for her.

Apparently thanks to the cleaning lady, it didn't need to be condemned now. It was spotless. The place looked like Ben, Molly thought at first glance, but even more it smelled like him, like his after-shave. It was a vast improvement over yeast and hops.

"Make yourself at home," he said as he headed for the kitchen.

Having almost no experience with men's apartments, Molly looked around curiously, realizing that it looked the way she imagined one would. It was bare of knickknacks, and the only things on the walls were an orange-and-blue Bronco pennant, a framed review of the opening of the first Boyd's Restaurant and a black-and-white photograph.

Molly stood in front of the picture to see it more closely. She couldn't help smiling at the sight of Ben in a leather motorcycle jacket, tight jeans and sunglasses.

"This other guy in the picture has to be related," she called to Ben.

"In my easy rider picture? It's my brother, Rick," he answered from the kitchen.

"Then where's your motorcycle?"

"Chopper, Molly, they were called choppers then."

"So where's your *chopper*?"

"In the repair shop where it spent most of its life until I junked it."

For a moment Molly remained staring at the photo, at Ben. His hair had been a little too long, his face younger, less angular. He looked the part of the rebel—very unlike he seemed now. And very sexy, though not as sexy as he was now.

Then realizing where her thoughts were headed, Molly spun around and took in the rest of the apartment.

There was a new stereo and an old television with a tennis racket propped against the stand. The stereo speakers were enormous, one of them balancing a video recorder and the other stacked with record albums. The furniture was brown leather—a button-tufted couch and one chair were positioned close around a coffee table where she could see the marks his heels had left. It was a comfortable place, not like home, not cozily decorated or thoughtfully planned, but she liked it just the same.

Ben ducked under the upper cupboards to talk to her through the open space above the stove top where he worked. "How about a little wine with our eggs?"

"Sounds good to me," she agreed.

Answering an urge, Molly kicked off her shoes and went into the kitchen. It was a compact space cluttered with more expensive-looking small appliances than she could put a name to.

Ben gave the skillet of eggs a quick stir, licked his thumb and opened the refrigerator. "I suppose champagne goes better with eggs—that's what we serve at Sunday brunch—but the closest I can come is a white zinfandel."

"I don't know enough about that stuff to be particular."

Molly watched as he stretched up to get wineglasses out of the cupboard above the range hood. He wore khaki slacks and a pale yellow shirt, the long sleeves rolled to his elbows. As he reached up, the shirt molded to his back, his muscular shoulders shifting beneath the fabric. Molly's gaze drifted down to where his slacks outlined a tight derriere.

She was suddenly very warm and forced herself to watch him pouring the wine. That wasn't much better, since she found the sight of his thick masculine wrists and big hands almost as arousing. She was grateful for the escape when he handed her both wineglasses, turned to spooning eggs onto two waiting plates, and said, "Everything gets done on the coffee table. Throw a couple of pillows on the floor, and I'll be right there."

She followed his instructions, sitting on the floor beside it, her back against the couch.

Ben brought the plates in, set them down and sat directly in front of Molly. She had expected him to sit on the other side of the table, either facing her or with his back to the couch, too. As it was, they were sharing the same side, and her bare toes were covered with his left calf.

He reached out and swept her hair back behind her shoulder. "How are you doing, lady?" he asked with an intimacy in his deep baritone that seemed to close the small space that separated them.

She couldn't answer his question because she didn't know how she was doing. Or *what* she was doing. "Thanks for everything you did tonight," she said instead. "It was nice not to be alone with that mess. Strange, but nice."

"Why strange?" He took a bite of his eggs.

Molly shrugged, pulling her glance away from the movement in the angular planes of his rawboned face as he chewed, a sight that did fluttery things to her stomach. She tried a forkful of her own eggs before answering him, finding that of all the senses that were coming to life in her so suddenly, a taste for food was not among them. "I'm not used to having help, to trusting or relying or counting on a man."

"Or on anyone else," he pointed out.

Again she shrugged. She hadn't really thought about it like that. "True." The atmosphere around them was lazy and serene. Nice. Molly sipped her wine and looked around the room. "I like your place."

Ben pushed his plate away. Enough was left on it to make it obvious his own appetite was nil. His glance followed the same path hers had taken. "Thanks, but it hardly looks like my place when it's this uncluttered." Then he looked back at Molly, his gaze so intense that she could feel it. "I like having you here."

Molly tried to resist looking back at him. He was so appealing, and she felt so many unusual things. But in the end she couldn't help it. She was hungry for the sight of him, for the warmth in his eyes, for the appreciation she always saw there. He twirled the stem of the wineglass between two thick fingers that looked too powerful to handle the delicate crystal without crushing it. Then he brought it to his mouth again, and she was mesmerized by the sight of his lips against the rim.

"Do you do it often?" Her words came out on their own, in a voice that was soft, breathy and a little afraid, surprising her.

He cocked his head, beetling his brow slightly in confusion. "Do I do what often?"

Molly looked off over her shoulder. "Have women in your apartment."

His chuckle came easily, his answer honestly. "No, I don't. What about you?"

"Me?"

A charged silence fell for a moment. Molly didn't understand his question, and she wasn't sure if that was because it wasn't clear or because her senses were demanding more of her attention than what he was saying to her. Every nerve in her body seemed to be slowly unsheathing and coming to life.

Ben reached one arm out and lightly grasped the back of her neck, raising her face to look into his. "You're a great—maybe even extraordinary—businesswoman, Molly. But I have a hunch that in the personal department you're a novice. Is that true?"

"A novice?" she repeated dimly. She wanted him to hold her. She couldn't make herself think about anything more serious than that. It was the strongest craving she had ever had.

"Making love, Molly." His words called her back from the warm abyss of her emotions. "It's not something you do . . . frivolously, is it?"

The term *making love* penetrated her sensuous reverie. Saying out loud what her thoughts were not putting a name to, what her body was yearning for, made her uncomfortable. "Is that what we're doing?" she hedged, taking a big swallow of wine. "I thought we were eating eggs."

"We aren't doing either." His eyes leveled so steadily on her made her feel even warmer. "Has a man ever made love to you?"

Molly swallowed hard. His bluntness made her nervous. The warmth of his hand against her nape made it difficult to answer his question. "He wasn't much of a man," she said in an unintentional whisper. "And it was a long time ago."

He slid his hand around to lay his palm against the side of her face. "Your first and only," he mused to himself. Then to her he said, "I'd like to be the second. And the last."

Molly closed her eyes and rested her face in his palm. She gave up any attempt to think straight. The sensations and emotions running through her were too powerful. Then she smiled slowly, languidly, and opened her eyes to look directly into the depths of his silver-gray ones. "Yes," was all she said.

He smiled back just as slowly, just as languidly. Then he leaned forward and took her mouth with his. His kiss was tender and tentative, as if he was testing her, warning her that he meant what he said. Then he sat back slightly and studied her face, seeming to gauge her reaction.

It touched Molly that he was so cautious. She reached a hand up, lightly smoothed one of his unruly, imposing eyebrows with her fingertips and then raised her chin just enough to kiss him back briefly, playfully, confirming what she had already agreed to.

His soft laughter said he understood. Then he stood up, pulling her with him, and showed her the way to the bedroom.

The room was lit only by the light from the living room. Not caring about anything but being with Ben, Molly noticed only that his bed was enormous. And then she was in his arms, and not another thought crossed her mind.

Ben held her with one arm around her back, his other hand cupping her head against the pressure of a kiss that was suddenly urgent and demanding. Molly met it in kind. She circled him with her own arms, filling her hands with the feel of the hard, powerful muscles of his back. Then his kiss lightened, and he pulled his arms away, unbuttoning the collar of her high-necked blouse, working his way down and tugging it from the waistband of her slacks. He ran his palms from her shoulders along the sensitive underside of her arms, forcing them down to slide her blouse off into a crumple at her bare feet. Her slacks went next, sliding easily from the slipperiness of the silky teddy she wore underneath.

Ben's mouth left hers to press into her neck, a soft chuckle sounding deep in his throat as he ran his hands down the teddy to her hips and back up again to the swell of her breast. A low moan followed Ben's chuckle, and his lips pressed to that tender mound of flesh. Heat radiated from his mouth to her skin and all through her body, eliciting a sigh from Molly that ended in a tiny groan of her own.

Then the teddy in a whispering swish joined the rest of Molly's clothes on the floor.

Naked before him, she shuddered slightly. Then she decided turnabout was fair play. She began to unbutton his shirt, but apparently she was too slow for him. Ben did most of it, shedding his clothes as urgently as if they were on fire.

In the dim light he was magnificent—tall, broad, hard, angular and very, very masculine. Molly sucked in her bottom lip at the glory of that first sight of him nude and reached both palms up his arms, to his shoulders and across the expanse of honed pectorals lightly thatched with hair. He drew in a quick breath when her touch trailed his hardened male nipples and grabbed her hands away in reflex as if the pleasure was too sharp to bear. He pressed her palms to his lips, kissing one and then the other. Without releasing her wrists, he led her to that big bed and lowered her to it with a mixture of gentleness and urgency.

Again his mouth found hers, his lips parted and then opened wide. Molly answered his hunger with one as great, her own mouth open and seeking, her tongue as persistent as his, until his hand found her breast and weakened her for a moment. Her body was alive in a joyous abandon that responded to his every touch, his every caress as wildly and uninhibitedly as if she had never known control at all, while inside she was a tight coil of need waiting to be sprung. Her back arched to his mouth as he found her nipple and took it to tease and suck and nip.

Impassioned as much by the feel of his body as by what he was doing to hers, Molly explored every bulging, straining mound of muscle, every tight depression of tendon, every long, hard sinew. She marveled in the feel of him. When his hand reached between her thighs, Molly gasped for air. She wanted him so much....

"Ben..." she whispered, her tone alone telling him how much she needed to feel him inside her.

He entered her slowly, carefully, the toll his consideration took showing in the cords that stood out along the length of his neck. Molly arched up to accept him. She couldn't stand another second of emptiness.

And then he was deeply imbedded inside her, pulsing with life, thrusting slowly at first, gently, tenderly, until neither of them could contain the passion they shared, climaxing at once in an extraordinary explosion that left them both weak and weighted and satiated.

Still joined, Ben rolled to his side, keeping Molly cradled between his legs and held tightly against his chest. "I'm falling in love with you, Molly," he said into her hair.

Molly squeezed her eyes closed and shook her head. "No, no, no," she whispered.

But even she didn't know if it was his feelings she was denying, or her own.

Chapter Seven

Bright sunshine coming through the thin drapes woke Molly up. For a moment she didn't know where she was. Lying on one side of an enormous bed, she looked around the room. It was starkly plain. There was a nightstand on the opposite side, with only a reading lamp and a clock radio. On the wall beside the bed was a nondescript dresser with an attached mirror nearly obscured by neckties draped over it, and in the corner was a wooden chair with a sport coat over the back. The sliding closet door was open to expose two tiers of clothes—shirts on top, pants on the bottom, and next to that was the door to an adjoining bathroom, also wide open.

Ben's bedroom.

The steady patter of a shower stopped suddenly, and before Molly could think what to do, the shower curtain slid open and there was Ben uninhibitedly, gloriously naked.

Reflex turned her head the other way, but curiosity brought it back when she heard him come into the bedroom. She didn't realize she hadn't been breathing until she saw that he had a towel slung low around his waist. Then she let out enough air to douse two dozen birthday candles. He didn't seem to be aware that he was being watched as he used a second towel to dry his hair.

Why did things look and feel so much different in the light of day? Molly had a two-fisted grip of the top of the sheet, holding it all the way to her throat. She didn't have the slightest idea what she should do.

Finally catching sight of her, Ben stopped, settling the towel like a horseshoe around his neck. "Good morning," he said, his hands still hanging onto the dangling ends of the towel, the easy smile on his face telling her he felt no discomfort in this situation.

Molly cleared her throat. "Morning," she mumbled back. It didn't help that he looked as appealing this morning as he had in the heat of passion the night before. His shoulders were wide and wet, his biceps bulged and glistened. Droplets of water clung to the sparse thatches of hair on his broad, muscular chest as well as to the straight line of golden fur that divided his narrow, flat belly. Was the towel around his waist lower than a moment before, or was it just that she hadn't noticed the shadowed indentation of his navel inches above it until now?

She watched rapidly as he used one end of the towel around his neck to dry the back of his head, wondering how he could look so good even with his hair mussed and sticking out in damp spikes. Then he used that same end to rub away the moisture on his chest as he came to sit on top of the sheet on his side of the bed.

He seemed totally unconcerned about the threat of exposure when he bent one knee up through the slit in the towel around his waist. Molly couldn't help but notice that massive muscular leg so close to where she was, or how absurdly sexy his big bare foot was as it rested against her hip with only the sheet separating them.

Ben stretched his arm out along the plain headboard and leaned slightly over her. "Why are you cowering under that sheet as if you're in mortal danger?"

"I'm not cowering," she lied.

"If your eyes get any wider, they're going to pop out of your head. It looks like cowering to me."

What was she supposed to do? Just sit up beside him, as bare breasted as he was, and have a conversation? "I..." she had to clear her throat again. "My other experience with...this...well, I was living at home with my grandparents and I still honored a curfew."

Ben's handsome face erupted into a broad grin. "Do you mean that this is the first time in your life you've actually spent the night with a man?"

Molly could feel red-hot heat suffusing her face. Apparently that was answer enough. Ben laughed. "God, that's sweet."

Molly didn't think it was sweet, at all. She felt ridiculous. And she didn't know what to say.

Ben seemed to be enjoying himself. One of his unruly eyebrows arched up high. "Was it always in the backseat of his souped-up Mustang?"

"No," she answered peevishly.

"Where, then? The laundry room at an unchaperoned party? His dorm room? The high-jump pit?"

"Very funny."

"That's where I did it."

"Not all of us were perverts," she announced loftily, but his good humor was infectious. She couldn't suppress a small smile at one thought. "The high-jump pit?"

He tilted his chin. "It was filled with sand—the closest I could come to a beach. Very romantic."

"Sounds like it."

"So where'd you do it?"

"He had an apartment. Boring, I know, compared to the high-jump pit."

"And I'll bet you were engaged already and everything."

"Are you making fun?"

"Affectionately." He proved it by dropping a quick kiss onto the tip of her nose. A drop of water fell from one of his unruly eyebrows to her forehead and made her frown at the tickling sensation. But she still didn't let go of the sheet.

Ben used the end of his damp towel to dry it for her. "So," he said with a mischievous look in his eyes. "When are you going to get up?"

"When you get out of here."

"No fun."

"Them's the breaks."

"Well, then, I guess I'd better tell you what our plans are for this weekend while I still have you captive."

"Excuse me?"

"Oh, and by the way, I called the hospital a little while ago to check on your driver. They wouldn't tell me anything except that he hadn't been admitted, so I looked up his number in the phone book and called his house. I got his wife, and she told me he has a broken arm, a stitched left temple and a few bruises but that he'll be fine."

"You did all that for me?" In her surprise the words slipped out.

He winked. "I'd like to crawl under that sheet and do a lot more for you."

Her grip tightened, but something inside her loosened. Maybe her heart. "It was really nice of you to think of it and call like that. Thank you."

He shrugged those big naked shoulders. "No big deal. Want to hear about our plans now?"

For a moment she watched him. His thoughtfulness touched her and at the same time struck her as odd. Everything he had done since she'd met him had been an unexpected kindness that seemed above and beyond the call of duty. It amazed her.

Was he too good to be true? Her mother had always said that about her father—that early in their marriage she had wondered if he was too good to be true. And then he had proved that he was. The thought took the tenderness out of her tone. "*We* don't have plans," she decreed.

"We, as in me, Karen, Melissa and Beth, do. I just thought you might like to come along."

"Excuse me?" she said again, more imperiously than before.

"Are you doing something rude under that sheet that you keep wanting me to excuse you for?"

"What plans are you talking about?" she said, rather than giving him the satisfaction of commenting on his teasing question.

"It's Labor Day weekend," he said as if that explained everything.

"I'm aware of that."

"My folks live in Evergreen. They have a big place—kind of the Colorado version of a Cape Cod family compound, complete with a guest house and a pool and a pond and a hot tub and about anything else you can name. For holidays, even little ones like Labor Day, my whole family traipses up there. My brother, who is dying to get a look at you, suggested I bring you up for the weekend, and all things considered, I thought it'd do Karen and her kids some good to get away, too. So I talked to her at work yesterday and she agreed."

Molly squinted at him. "Going behind my back to get Karen to agree to this before you even tell me is really devious and underhanded."

He smiled. "I know."

"Don't you have to work this weekend?"

"I'll go in until the dinner crowd is under control tonight and then hand things over to my manager. We'll head up about seven, while it's still light out, and get up there by eight. So what do you say? Are we going with or without you?"

"You know if I say without, Karen won't go, and I'll feel guilty that she and the girls didn't do something they want to."

"Yep. And they'll sit around your house feeling miserable. Karen will be an easy target if her husband decides to make another impromptu visit like he did yesterday morning—she told me about it—whereas if they're in Evergreen he won't have any idea how or where to get hold of them. But of course it's entirely up to you."

"You know those nice things I was thinking about you a few minutes ago because you called the hospital? Well, they're history."

"Were you thinking nice things about me?" Without any warning he bent over and kissed the tip of her breast through the sheet. Molly gasped with sudden pleasure. Then he defended himself in a husky voice, "I just wanted to spend time with you."

Molly closed her eyes and fought to douse the sparks that ignited desire every bit as hot and demanding as the night before. Eleven years of abstinence and now she couldn't go twelve hours. She should say no to this weekend with him no matter what it cost Karen and the kids. But a part of her—that part that still sizzled—didn't want to say no.

Big trouble. She was in big, big trouble.

She felt him slide down on the bed and lean over her, his arms on either side of her head, his face only inches away from hers. When she opened her eyes, his were right there, staring at her, all the teasing gone from his expression.

"I don't know what's in your head or your past that's making you think you have to put the skids on the attraction between us, but whatever it is, fight it. Together you and I can have something special, if you'll just let it happen."

It was hard for her to realize it, but she wanted to believe that. She wanted to believe him.

It wasn't as if she was doing what her mother and her sister had done—it wasn't as if she was trusting him. She was just indulging herself for a little while—

like binging in the middle of a diet. As long as you knew what you were doing, knew you could go right back on the diet when the binge was over, what harm was there?

"I won't hurt you," he vowed in a soft, sincere voice.

"I won't let you," she answered him, and hoped it was true. For a moment their eyes locked, and then Molly changed the subject. "Are you sure your family wants four extra last-minute guests?"

"My mother was thrilled. The more the merrier."

"Then I guess you win this round, Boyd," she conceded.

He frowned down at her. "I hope you mean that as if it's a game and not a fight."

But Molly didn't answer that. Instead she scrunched her face up into a grimace. "The laundry room at an unchaperoned party? Did you lie on piles of dirty clothes?"

Ben studied her, searching her face for a clue to what was going on in her mind, but in the end he conceded to her return to the lighter subject. "Didn't you know the smell of sweaty socks is an aphrodisiac to a teenage boy?"

"Yuck."

Once again he kissed the tip of her nose. "I suppose you're going to make me leave the room before you'll get up, aren't you?"

"Please," she said politely.

He rolled to his side, braced on one elbow and raked his eyes down her sheet-covered body and back again. "Okay, okay. If I don't have any other choice." He got up, not bothering to straighten or resecure the towel around his waist, and headed out the bedroom door. As he did, he dropped his head far back and said, "What I wouldn't give for a keyhole."

"Put your seatbelts on, too," Ben called to Molly and Karen just before he got behind the wheel of his Jaguar. Having invited Melissa and Beth to ride with him up to Evergreen, he had already made sure they were belted in tight.

"Nice man," Karen mused as she followed orders and fastened hers.

"Mmm," Molly agreed noncommittally as she started her Toyota and backed out of the driveway into line behind Ben.

"I fell asleep about ten last night," Karen offered out of the blue.

Molly knew what was coming. She didn't say anything.

"And I was up by five this morning."

"Nightmares or adrenaline?" Molly asked, trying to avoid the direction she knew her sister was headed.

"Both. I got up and went downstairs to make coffee. It surprised me when I passed your bedroom and the door was still open because you weren't home." There was amusement in Karen's voice.

"I hope you didn't worry."

Karen laughed. "I figured if you had had an accident or something, I would have been notified."

"Actually there was an accident," Molly said, again veering off the subject. She relayed the story of the previous night's wreck.

"So Ben was with you through the whole thing?" Karen persisted.

Molly craned around to check oncoming traffic before merging onto the highway behind the vintage

Jaguar. "He was a big help. No, to be honest, he did more than I did. I was kind of at a loss. The last accident the company had was just after I started working there, and Grandpa handled everything."

"Nice man, don't you think?" Karen reiterated.

"Mmm," Molly said again.

"And then you spent the night with him," Karen surmised bluntly since her sister was obviously not going to offer the information.

They had been telling each other every intimate detail of their lives for too long to stop now, so Molly just laughed and gave in. "And then I spent the night with him."

"Good for you."

Molly groaned.

"Not good for you?"

Molly groaned again.

"*Too* good for you," Karen concluded, and then sighed. "Oh, Molly."

"What, 'oh, Molly'?" she mimicked.

"It isn't possible for it to be *too* good."

"Of course it is. Actually, that's just when to watch out. Perfect men, perfect marriages—and then what happens? The hard fall."

"So instead you keep your guard up and never let anyone in. Is that the alternative?"

"Works for me."

"Except now. I know you. If you slept with him, you've let your guard down."

"Nope. I'm just binging," Molly said so confidently that there didn't seem to be a doubt.

"Then you're nuts. Ben Boyd is perfect. He's one of the nicest guys I've ever met."

Molly's laugh this time was ironic. "As I recall, Grandma and Grandpa said repeatedly that that was just what they thought about our father. They were stunned to find the real John Northrup beneath the facade. I also seem to remember hearing that perfect stuff once or twice about Carl, too," she reminded her gently.

"So you think that everything we know about Ben is just fake?" Karen asked dubiously.

Molly shrugged. "No, not fake. Just temporary. It's true for now, while he's in the mood. I'm just saying that what you see now is not what you get in the end. It can't be trusted."

Karen didn't say anything for a few minutes. "That's hard to refute from where I'm standing," she admitted softly.

Molly took her eyes off the road to smile at her sister and shrug a little helplessly. "They're just shallow, Karen. Maybe it's something in the testosterone." What Molly had intended as glib had come out sounding sad. She tried to finish on an upbeat note. "Maybe we're all better off once we admit it and prepare ourselves for it."

"What about love, Molly?"

Molly didn't want to think about that. It had occurred to her this morning that love was like the flu— you caught it whether you wanted it or not, whether you did everything to avoid it or not. That scared her.

When she didn't answer Karen's question, her sister went on. "Well, I think Ben is a really nice guy, and you're crazy if you let him get away."

Molly didn't want to be convinced. To be convinced was to be vulnerable, and she was already too much of that. "Like I said—I'm just binging. They all get away in the end."

To get to the Boyd home nestled against the side of a mountain, they crossed a stone bridge over a meandering brook. The house was a two-story combination of logs and stone that stretched out a full city block and yet meshed with the pine trees and rock formations that were its backdrop. Around the semicircular drive that swept all the way to the front door was a lush green lawn kept in surgically precise condition with the tractor mower that stood beside a three-car detached garage. Flower gardens edged the stone-terraced side of the brook, filled an oval in the lee of the drive and surrounded two iron sentries on either side of the front door.

Ben drove across the bridge honking what Molly assumed was an announcement of their arrival. But the only welcoming party to appear was a big springer spaniel with green boots tied around all four paws. And he came at a snail's pace.

"Hello, Laddy," Ben called the dog, slapping his thighs as if it would inspire the old animal to a trot. It didn't. Laddy came in his own good time. "He's harmless," Ben told Beth as she made a beeline for the dog.

"How come he's wearing shoes?" Molly heard her oldest niece ask as she headed around to the back of her car and popped the trunk.

"The pads of his paws are worn off—that's how old he is," Ben explained.

"Beth will be in heaven," Karen told him as she went around Molly and joined Ben. "She's wild for animals."

"There's three cats and a kitten, too."

Molly bent over the trunk and took a hold of the old blue suitcase that held the girl's things. But before she could hoist it out, Ben called to her.

"Leave those, honey. We can bring them in later."

She stopped short at the endearment and looked up to meet her sister's eyes and see the grin on her face. Karen might have found it amusing, but Molly wasn't sure she liked the affectionate address, even though it did make her feel that rush of warmth she was beginning to associate automatically with Ben.

"Well, it's about time," came the sound of an older woman's voice from the front door.

"Hi, my little Margie," Ben greeted, obviously teasing her with the use of her first name. Then, in three steps, he closed the space between himself and the short, slightly overweight woman with the stylish gray hair. He gave her a hug and kiss, and then, with his arm around her shoulders, he introduced Molly, Karen and the girls to his mother.

Marge Boyd didn't look anything at all like her son. Her features, like her body, were rounded and smooth. She smiled a relaxed welcome at them all. "Everybody's out back. There's iced tea or wine and munchies if you're hungry. But whatever you do, don't mention the new satellite dish out there. Ed's dying for any excuse to get in front of the boob tube where he's been glued ever since we got the thing."

Karen and the girls followed Marge into the house. As Molly brought up the rear, Ben put his arm around her and pulled her into his side to whisper in her ear. "I know she's a little dated, but we like her."

They passed through the entryway into a large living room furnished with two loud, floral early American sofas, three chairs, a coffee table and a baby grand piano. The space was littered with toys, purses, diaper bags, shoes, a few suitcases and the various debris of houseguests. The kitchen came next, an enormous, open space so starkly modern that it had obviously just been remodeled.

"I know, Ben," Marge called back to her son as they went through, "you're dying to get into my new kitchen. You can do dinner tomorrow night and brunch Monday morning. Every other meal around here this weekend is going to be catch-as-catch-can. I'm on strike from cooking."

"You should have told me ahead of time," he countered teasingly. "Then I wouldn't have had to pack the stomach pump."

Marge's answering laugh was loud, boisterous and uninhibited—just like Ben's.

Wide glass sliding doors opened from there onto an expansive slate-tiled back patio shaded by trees and the slope of the mountain. To the left was a small pool, to the right a tennis court and directly in front was a volleyball-badminton net. Bright yellow cushioned redwood patio furniture was haphazardly positioned around snack tables and a playpen where three babies of nearly the same age vied for a set of plastic donut rings.

"Hey, Ben, I was beginning to think you weren't going to get up here!" yelled a man who sat in one of the loungers, a woman held playfully captive across his lap.

"That's Rick and his wife, Tammi," Ben said, introducing them.

Molly recognized the man from the picture in Ben's apartment. "The other Easy Rider," she commented, and made Rick and his wife both laugh.

Ben squeezed the spot where Molly's neck curved into her shoulder and said in an aside, "That's how they met. Tammi had dreams of being a motorcycle mama."

"Yeah, and all I got to be was a mama," Tammi complained good-naturedly.

"See that tow-headed kid with the water pistol and the two-year-old eating what looks to be a cricket? Those two and that little bald baby about to have her first birthday are theirs."

With that Tammi jumped up to save the cricket from ingestion.

"I made vegetable dip," offered a younger version of Marge who stood at the table laden with snacks and drinks. Ben guided Molly there, motioning Karen with them for introductions to his sister, also named Karen, and the discussion turned to how to differentiate between the two Karens. It was settled that Molly's sister would be Karen D., while Ben's would be Karen K.—for Kline. When Karen K.'s husband Bill snuck up behind his wife and swatted her on the rear end, he got introduced, too.

"Those other two babies in the playpen are theirs. The Boyd family's first set of twins."

"Now me!" called a woman who looked much like Ben and Rick. She sat in a lounge chair, looking up from a magazine.

"This one is Tordia," Ben announced in what sounded more like some kind of animal call than a name, making his sister grimace.

"You know I hate it when you call me that," she complained in a way that said she didn't hate it at all.

"Actually, we call her Tory. The Tordia came from Karen not being able to say Victoria. Those are her two kids playing tennis with their dad, Gib, over on the courts."

"How 'bout your old man?" A very attractive man stood and came to them. He had a full head of thick silver hair around an older version of Ben's face.

"Hi, Pop. This is the light of my life, Molly Mercer, and her sister, Karen Dune."

The introduction embarrassed Molly, but no one seemed to notice.

Ed Boyd winked broadly at his son and then said to Molly, "Ever see what you can get on TV with a satellite dish?"

"Ed," Marge chastized from across the patio where she shouldn't have been able to hear.

"Damn woman buys me a present and then gets mad when I use it. Make any sense to you?"

But before Molly could think of an answer, Marge said, "I didn't buy it so you'd have an excuse to be rude."

A sly smile curled one side of Ed's mouth as he said confidentially, yet loudly enough to make sure his wife heard, "She bought it so she could watch male strippers."

Marge threw a stuffed animal at him and hit him in the back of the head. "You weren't supposed to tell that."

With the introductions complete, Beth and Melissa joined the tennis game, and Karen wandered off to admire the babies, falling naturally into mother talk with Karen K. and Tammi. Taking Molly's free hand,

Ben pulled her with him to a glider where he sat so close to her that their thighs formed a seam. He stretched his arm along the back of the cushioned seat and settled in close to her as naturally as if they belonged together.

The evening passed pleasantly on the Boyds' slate patio as the family caught up with what had happened in everyone's life since the last time they had talked. Teasing and loving concern were the order of the day.

By the time Ben's family began to drift inside to put kids and babies to bed and watch movies on Ed's new satellite dish, Molly felt as comfortable as if she were at home. It surprised her, and she attributed it to the warmth of the entire Boyd family.

"Do you usually bring friends with you when you come up here?" she couldn't help asking when she and Ben were left alone on the glider.

"Friends," he repeated. "As in men or as in women?"

Of course it was 'as in women.' For some reason it was very important to Molly to know, but she said, "Both," rather than admit it.

"No," he answered obliquely, amusement sounding in his voice.

Molly wanted to know that one too much not to play into his hands. "No as in no men or no as in no women?"

"Neither."

"Never?"

"I didn't say that."

Molly sighed and looked into the distance. The sky was obliterated by trees, leaving it very dark. She spotted a firefly and concentrated on it.

After a few minutes of silence, Ben chuckled. "Why don't you say it like this—how many women have you brought up here with you before? I love this jealous streak you have. It's the only way I get a glimpse of what you're really feeling about me." He nuzzled her neck, chuckling as he did. "Well, that and last night in..."

"Shh..." she berated him.

Ben's laughter filled the night air. Then he whispered, "Nobody's out here but us chickens. And you're the biggest chicken of them all."

"I beg your pardon?"

"Because you're too scared to just ask me what you want to know."

"Okay, wise guy. How many women have you brought up here before me?"

"Six hundred and forty-nine." He laughed at his own humor, which Molly did not find amusing at all, and then said, "The answer is the same as the number of lovers you had before me."

"One," she said, wondering why it bothered her to know even one had preceded her.

"And after her it's a wonder they didn't ban me from ever doing it again."

That made her feel better. Good enough in fact to joke back. "Body odor," she stated as if she already knew it was true.

He squeezed her so hard that he hunched her shoulders forward. "Now who's a wise guy? Actually her body was what got me into trouble. My brother and brothers-in-law couldn't keep their eyes off it."

She rolled her eyes, but before she could change the subject Ben went on.

"Of course, as Rick puts it, she didn't have the brains to tie her own shoes, but in a bikini no one but me noticed that."

"Oh, right, and you did," she said skeptically.

"Absolutely. The clincher was on the way up here when we passed a license plate from Maryland. She said, 'Mary Land. What's that?' I thought she must be joking, but she was dead serious. She'd never heard of it."

Molly laughed. "Okay, you win. Cut the baloney."

"No baloney. It's the truth. She was dumb. You can ask Rick. Just don't do it when Tammi can hear or it'll start everyone arguing about that Fourth of July."

Molly really didn't know if he was putting her on. But rather than pursue it, she reminded herself that she had no reason to care about any other woman in Ben's life. After all, she was just his binge, the same as he was just hers.

"It's really beautiful up here," she said to change the subject, taking a deep breath of pine-scented mountain air in hopes that it would make the sudden glum feelings she had go away.

He kissed the side of her neck, his breath warm. "You should see it when the snow starts to fly. It looks like a postcard. Christmas is amazing."

For a split second Molly had a twinge at the thought that by then someone else could be sitting where she was. She didn't like it, so rather than say any more about it, she said, "Is your father retired?"

"Last year. He was an accountant."

She didn't seem able to avoid bad feelings tonight.

When Molly said nothing, Ben pulled slightly back to look at her in the faint light coming from the house. "Why does that make you go stiff?"

Molly shrugged the stiffness away. "No reason."

"Your father was an accountant before he went to San Diego, wasn't he?"

She dropped her head back to look at the stars through the small space between the treetops. "Did you grow up here?" she asked instead of answering him.

"I did." Then he went back to the subject she was avoiding. "So do you have some deep-seated resentment toward accountants?"

"I like your dad. In fact I like all your family."

"And you don't want to talk about yours."

Molly shrugged. "There's nothing to talk about. You knew my father. You liked him, I didn't."

"I'd like to understand why," he said sincerely.

Against his arm she shook her head. "This is one of the most peaceful, beautiful nights I've ever spent. I don't want to think about him, much less talk about him and ruin it."

For a moment more silence elapsed, but finally Ben said, "I can't argue with that." And then he leaned over and kissed her.

His mouth was warm and slightly moist, familiar now and yet still new and exciting to Molly. He kissed her slowly, tenderly, like young lovers on a porch swing. It was nice, sweet. She sighed into it and laid her palm against his cheek, feeling the beginning roughness of his beard's growth. She felt cherished, wanted, contented. Wouldn't it be wonderful if it could go on forever?

But it couldn't, and she had to remember that.

She concentrated on his kiss instead, on the way it was rapidly deepening, on the way his lips were opening, on matching it by opening her own, meeting his tongue as if it were an old friend.

She felt the cool night air against her bare stomach as his hand slid underneath her V-neck T-shirt, drawing an involuntary gasp when he found her breast beneath her bra.

She was instantly filled with desire. She circled the breadth of his chest with her arms, feeling the play of his muscles beneath his cotton shirt. He pulled her closer, and Molly slipped down to nearly lie on the vinyl cushion of the glider. His thigh was between her legs, riding up to that spot that felt so desperately empty. She had to stop wanting him so much. She had to stop....

Molly drew a deep breath and turned her head away from his kiss, her body away from the magic of his hand on her bare flesh. "I can't do this." The difficulty of forcing words through a throat constricted with passion made her voice sound choked.

Ben dropped his forehead to her collarbone. "You're right. This is as bad as two teenagers fooling around under their parents' noses. Tacky."

Molly gulped air and let him think that was why she had put the skids on her own desire for him.

Ben groaned low in his throat. "Maybe coming up here wasn't such a good idea. It didn't occur to me that spending the weekend together here meant sleeping apart. I don't suppose you'd like to go in right now and tell my folks you've gotten suddenly sick and are in imminent need of my taking you back to Denver?"

She had gotten suddenly sick, she realized, but it was purely emotional. It struck her like lightning that she desperately wanted forever to be possible, and yet she just didn't believe it was. The disappointment made her ill.

"Molly?" Ben called her back from her thoughts when she hadn't responded. "Are you all right?"

She swallowed the lump in her throat and tried to sound glib. "Just catching my breath." But what she was really doing was fighting the sting of hot tears in her eyes. Why did she always have to want the impossible?

Ben sat up and pulled her with him. He ducked his head down to peer directly into her face, but that blocked the light from the kitchen's sliding door. Instead he tipped it up with a finger under her chin. "I love you, Molly," he said softly, sincerely.

Molly swallowed with difficulty and forced a smile. "It's just this thin mountain air," she quipped, making light of it.

"Wrong."

"We better go in. It's getting cool out here." She tried to stand up and make her escape, but Ben stopped her with a hand on her arm.

The silence between them was suddenly palpable.

Then he seemed to decide not to push what she was so obviously trying to avoid. He took her hand and pulled her with him as he stood. "Come on, I'll show you your room."

The sad note in his voice clenched Molly's heart. She just wished she could believe him, believe in him.

Chapter Eight

The smell of mountain air had been too good to close out the night before, and as a result sunshine poured in through the open drapes of two east windows to wake Ben up early Sunday morning. He didn't mind. It wasn't often that he got up to Evergreen, and he didn't want to sleep the day away.

Rolling onto his back, he clasped his hands behind his head and slowly came awake to old familiar sights.

This same room had been his as a kid. It wasn't much different now than it had been then. Even the glossy blue-and-silver psychedelic wallpaper he had picked out when he was fifteen was still up on the wall at the foot of the bed.

There weren't any bad memories of his childhood, he thought as he scanned the room, his gaze falling on the tennis trophies, yearbooks and assorted science fiction and comic books on the shelves his father had built for him, on the tower of tennis-ball cans he had stacked in one corner, on the small bank shaped like a safe that still sat on the bureau.

In one way or another, his parents had given their children a strong sense of themselves. They had built their confidence, had made them feel secure and supported enough in this home base to try their wings when the need surfaced. And now Ed and Marge Boyd could look at four people who were productive, successful, happy adults. That must be a great feeling of accomplishment. One Ben was just beginning to realize he'd like for himself.

He would like to have kids of his own lying in a room he had provided for them, a safe cocoon where they could grow and blossom and feel the same things he had felt here in this room. And he knew who he'd like to do it with.

Molly Mercer.

Ben yawned and stretched.

Even though she wouldn't admit it, he believed she shared his feelings. But she was fighting it like crazy, and he didn't understand that.

She responded to him like a dry duck on a hot summer day took to water. And yet as soon as she realized what was happening, she put the skids on it and tried to run the other way.

Maybe she just wasn't used to good things happening between a man and a woman.

But she'd have to *get* used to it, because he wanted Molly Mercer. And it had nothing to do with thin mountain air.

The Boyds were all genuinely nice people, Molly thought as she sat on the grass beside the tennis court watching what Ben had proclaimed the First Annual Labor Day Tennis Tournament on Sunday afternoon. Ed had taken her sister as his doubles partner, and they had just been beaten by Ben and Tammi.

Molly's gaze stayed on the older man and Karen as they came through the gate and headed for the pool. Ed's arm was around Karen's shoulders. She was laughing and jabbing him in the ribs with her elbow in answer, no doubt, to yet another of the good-natured, innocent propositions he teased all the women with. Molly could only assume he made everyone feel the way he did her—very flattered, very feminine and very attractive. The fact that he was joking didn't alter that.

As Molly watched them join the rest of the Boyds and Melissa and Beth in and around the pool, she had a strong sense of déjà vu. Not that she had ever had this experience before, but it was something she had fantasized about often as a child. A normal family. Mother, father, kids, all together in one place loving one another.

She had envied her friends their families and for a long, long time imagined one for herself. Even now as an adult there were some times, especially at holidays, when she had wished for that feeling of warmth and closeness the Boyds took for granted.

For a moment she felt a wave of sadness. For herself. For Karen. For Karen's kids, for whom history was repeating itself.

But then she pushed the thoughts and feelings away. She and Karen and the girls had one another. That was all that was really important.

With a concentrated effort she turned back to the court.

"Winners and new champeens!" Ben called like a fight announcer, holding his racket high with both arms over his head.

He wore a tight tank top that revealed his developed biceps, shoulders and the swells of his pectorals. A pair of bright red jogging shorts exposed most of his thighs. Molly enjoyed the sight as he came to her, sitting on one hip beside her, his other leg bent up high to brace his forearm as he leaned toward her on his hand.

"To the victor comes the spoils," he misquoted, kissing her bare elbow where it jutted toward him from her arms circling her updrawn knees. He slid his sunglasses to the top of his head, leaving a damp white line across the bridge of his nose.

"I'm the spoils? I beg your pardon?" she said, laughing.

"Want a big hug?" He held his arm out and leaned closer. Sweat glazed his skin in an even sheen.

Molly angled away from him. "No, thanks."

He sat up and crossed his legs Indian fashion before he pulled the tank top up and off. Then he dropped his head far back and used the shirt to dry the arch where his Adam's apple poked out like a knuckle in his thick, corded neck. Still using the shirt for a towel, he swiped under both arms before tossing it into a heap in front of him. Then he plucked a long piece of grass to clamp between his teeth and braced back on his elbows. "Great up here, isn't it?"

"Mmm," Molly agreed, her throat suddenly congested in response to the feast her eyes had just consumed.

"Think anybody would notice if we snuck in and took a shower together?"

Tempting. Very tempting. Molly swallowed some of that congestion. "Oh, only one or two or ten people."

"And I suppose that would bother you?"

She held her thighs tightly together. "You're all talk," she teased back in a voice she hadn't intended to be so husky.

Ben smiled wickedly and warned her, "You don't want to call this bluff."

She changed the subject. "What are you cooking for us tonight?"

"Steak and salad for us big guys, hot dogs for the twinkies."

"You Boyds have an interesting terminology for kids. So far today I've heard them called rug rats, twinkies and twits."

"Yeah, but we love them all just the same."

She knew that. She had seen it clearly. Children being cherished, valued. It was all part of her old fantasy. "I hate to tell you, but Melissa and Beth are more likely to eat steak than hot dogs."

He took the blade of grass from his mouth and drew a line with it down the sensitive underside of her arm. "No problem." He sounded distracted. Then he arched up and kissed the same spot. "How can you sit out here in this heat all day and still smell good?"

Chills went all the way through her. Molly tried to disguise what he was rousing in her by being glib. "Horses sweat, men perspire and women merely glow," she recited.

Ben laughed and kissed her again. "That sounded very Victorian."

"Besides I never budged out of the shade," she admitted.

"I'd like to get you worked up into a sweat." He did a fast sit-up and pulled off first his disreputable-looking tennis shoes and then his socks, tossing them all onto his shirt and cooling his big bare feet in the lawn.

Molly realized she was staring at those feet and the bony, hairy ankles above them. She forced herself to look up at his face. Somehow, it seemed less intimate. Unfortunately it was no less arousing. His hair was dampened to a dark wheat color, his rawboned face looked more finely chiseled beneath the deeper tan that the day's tennis had netted him. She couldn't stay here, looking at him and listening to his innuendos a moment longer. Not without calling that bluff of his. She sprang to her feet.

"Actually I'm hotter than I thought." It was a bad choice of words.

Ben laughed appreciatively.

Molly explained in a hurry, "I think I'll take a shower before dinner."

Ben gathered his discarded clothes and stood up, too. "Admit it, Mercer, you're wild for me."

Molly gave him an imitation of Greta Garbo. "I'm wild for you. Simply wild."

Ben just smiled smugly. "I know. Now if I could just get you to believe it."

While Ben coerced the older children to join the babies by going to bed that night, Molly insisted that she do the kitchen cleanup. Karen joined in, and between the two of them they conquered all protests.

It didn't take long, and as Molly finished up at the sink, her sister went to the sliding-glass door to go back outside.

"Oh," the simple word seemed to rush out of her mouth.

Molly looked up in time to see Karen stop in her tracks. "What's the matter?" Then she glanced out the window over the sink in the direction Karen was staring.

The couples had all paired up on the patio. Marge and Ed sat in facing lawn chairs, his feet in her lap where she softly massaged them, Rick and Tammi were lying together in one of the loungers, Tory sat at her husband Gib's side, her arm draped over his knees, and Karen Kline sat in her husband Bill's lap, her arms around his neck, her head resting on top of his.

For a moment both Molly and Karen stood there, frozen, staring silently. What they saw could have been a Valentine's Day card.

Karen sighed. The sound was raspy in the quiet kitchen. "I never thought it could be so hard to watch other people in love. I . . ." Molly could tell what she was thinking even before she finished. "I wonder if it's a long distance call from Evergreen to Denver."

Molly turned back to scrubbing out the sink. "I don't know," she answered softly, not wanting to look at the mesmerized, forlorn expression on her sister's face any more than she did at the sight just outside.

Suddenly, as if she had made a decision, Karen spun away. "I'll ask the operator. If it is, I'll call collect," she said more strongly than Molly had heard her say anything since her marital mess had begun.

And then she left Molly alone in the kitchen with that scene of love and closeness just outside the window.

She rinsed the stainless steel sink and used a dish towel to dry it, each stroke a swipe. Then she polished the faucet so hard that she made a little scratch in the chrome.

But she didn't look out that window directly in front of her. She had seen enough.

With her jaw set, she folded the dish towel as efficiently, as crisply, as precisely as a drill sergeant teaching new recruits. Then she slapped it over the towel rack on the inside of a cupboard door and slammed it closed.

She turned away from the sink to see if she had missed anything and realized something was sticking out of the refrigerator door. Storming over to the appliance, she yanked it open, jammed the plastic bag in around the cherries it held and shoved the door closed again.

Then her eyes strayed back to the phone.

Was Karen on it? Had she called Carl? Of course she had. One look out that back door and ...

Molly didn't want to think about that.

When one of her hands cramped, Molly realized for the first time that they were both clenched into fists. Instantly she opened them up, her fingers splayed like sunbursts.

Lotion. That's what she needed. Her hands were so rough.

There was a bottle on the windowsill above the sink.

Molly went back, staring steadfastly at the black-and-white tile checkerboard backsplash. The lotion was in a black dispenser with the letters in white above a sprig of yellow daisies. Molly reached for it. As she did, the flash of a match outside caught her eye.

On the patio Ed was standing up to light several citronella flares. One by one they threw dim light like halos around each couple.

Molly's gaze went from one to the other to the other, ending on Marge as Ed sat back down and put his feet in her lap again. She couldn't tell what the older woman said to him, but whatever it was, it made everyone laugh. In apparent revenge he tried tickling her side with his big toe. Marge gave him a broad wink, and his toe went up a little higher before she gently slapped it down again.

Molly felt stiff and uncomfortable. Maybe she didn't like the Boyds, either.

No, that wasn't true. She liked them very much. They were nice people. Lucky people. They had what she had always wanted.

The sound of Ben's deep voice saying a firm, last good-night to one of the kids penetrated Molly's trance.

Her mouth was suddenly dry. Too dry.

Ben would come into the kitchen and see her and want her to join him and the rest of his family. He would take her hand the way he had last night, the way he had all day today whenever they were together, and pull her to the glider that seemed to be out there just waiting for them. He would make sure they sat close together. His arm would go around her. He would hold her tight against his side and every so often, even as they talked with everyone else out there, he'd squeeze her shoulder and hug her even closer. And it would feel good. Too good.

Karen was in the other room, probably making up with Carl. The whole Boyd clan was out on the patio snuggling with their respective partners. She and Ben were the only ones left.

Molly could hear the thwap of his sandals on the steps as he came downstairs.

After a while everyone else would go in to their beds and leave them alone the way they had last night. Ben would nuzzle her neck. He'd say things, funny things, touching things, intimate things that would start the sizzle. Then he'd tip her face up to his and kiss her. And it would feel good. Too good.

To anyone who saw it, they would look close, caring, loving, inseparable. Just the way those other couples looked.

It might even begin to feel that way. It might even begin to seem perfect. And then she'd believe it and be lost.

She heard him reach the bottom landing. His steps became muffled in the thick shag carpeting.

As if she was cornered, Molly searched for a way out. The sliding doors led to the patio. The opposite direction led to the living room and Ben. But there, next to the refrigerator was another door that led to a mud porch off the side of the house.

It didn't take Molly more than three seconds to make her escape.

Ben paused for a minute halfway down the hallway and arched his back until it cracked. Giving horse rides was tough work. He tucked his navy blue T-shirt into the waistband of his corduroy shorts and headed for the kitchen to fix himself a tall glass of iced tea. Then he'd get Molly cozied up with him on the glider. Paradise.

He got only as far as the door to the den.

"Ben?"

The voice was so soft that he wasn't immediately sure who was calling to him. He stopped and leaned in. Karen Dune was sitting behind the desk in near total darkness. He walked over and perched on the corner. "What's up?"

"Are the kids asleep yet?" she asked, her voice a little shaky.

"I sincerely doubt it. Are you all right? You sound kind of down."

She sighed and sat back in his father's big leather chair. A dim glow of light from the hallway fell on her face. She looked tired. "I'm really a coward."

Ben chuckled. "Okay. If you say so."

"I need to ask Molly a favor, and she's not going to like my reason for it, so I'm taking the coward's way out and asking if you'll do it."

"Ah, I get it. Let's have it, then."

"I want to borrow her car, pack the girls up right now and go home."

"Oh," Ben said, slightly taken aback. "Did something happen that made you want to leave?"

"Oh, no," she was quick to reassure him. "It doesn't have anything to do with wanting to leave. I love it here. I love your family. But, well, everybody is out on the patio sitting all snuggled up together, and it really hit me hard. I came in here and called my husband. The home I'm going back to is my own."

Glad to hear that, he reached over and squeezed her shoulder. "Good for you."

She didn't look as if she totally agreed with that. "I hope it will be. I hope we can work this out."

Ben thought about it for a second, wondering what kind of flak he was putting himself in line for. But in the end he took Molly's car keys out of his pocket and handed them to Karen. "You're in luck. I had to move her car out of the way when Rick went for ice cream. I'm giving you the go-ahead. Leave Molly to me."

Karen looked more dubious about that than she had about the future of her marriage. "Molly isn't going to approve of this."

It wasn't news to him, but Ben pretended ignorance. "She isn't going to like what? Your borrowing her car or going back to your husband?"

"The car won't matter."

"So were you thinking of getting a divorce just to please Molly?"

That made her smile a little. "No, it's just that for all I know, she may be right about this and I'm only headed for more heartache by going back. You know—fool me once shame on you, fool me twice shame on me."

"You know what I think? I think that if you don't go back and give it your best shot, you'll never know if your marriage could have worked out. You'll always wonder and you'll always feel as if you didn't explore every option. There's no shame in doing whatever you have to to keep your family together."

Apparently his pep talk was just what she needed. Karen smiled. "Thanks. You're right. If I let pride keep me from doing this—my own or Molly's—I'll never know." She took the keys. "You're sure you don't mind telling Molly?"

Ben couldn't help laughing wryly at that, but he reassured her, anyway. "I can handle it. Just drive safely. If you wreck her car, she'll kill me," he teased. "Is she still in the kitchen?"

"That's where I left her."

Ben pushed off the desktop and headed for the door. "If I were you, I'd make a quick getaway."

"Good idea. Thanks again."

"Don't mention it. Good luck." He left the den and went into the kitchen, wondering how to break the news to Molly.

But the kitchen was empty.

One glance outside told him Molly wasn't on the patio, so he poked his head out the sliding door.

"Has anybody seen Molly?"

Tory's husband Gib pointed toward the tennis courts. "I thought I saw her go out through the mud porch a few minutes ago and head that way."

"Aha. She must be dying to get me alone," he said as he weaved his way through the lawn furniture.

"Sure," Rick called from behind him. "That's why she snuck out the side door without you."

Ben waved off his brother's remark and stepped out into the grass in the direction of the courts.

The air was just cool enough to be comfortable. A full moon shone through the space between the tree-tops, casting a silver glow on the tips of the boughs and aspen branches. The farther Ben got from the house, the softer grew the voices of his family, so that by the time he reached the tennis courts only an occasional boisterous laugh drifted through the otherwise silent night.

He didn't see Molly until he went onto the courts. She was standing on the outside, opposite the direction from which he had come.

"Hey, lady," he called when he first spotted her. "What are you doing out here?"

She didn't answer him. He wasn't sure if she had heard him, though he didn't know why she wouldn't have. But he waited until he had crossed the court, gone out the other gate and was standing beside her to repeat himself.

She was leaning her forehead against the high chain link fence that surrounded the courts, her fingers hooked through the links, staring at the ground. Her forehead was puckered with a forlorn frown, and she still didn't answer him.

Some of the teasing left Ben's tone of voice. "With the way you shun tennis, this is the last place I would have expected you to be."

Molly laughed a sad, ironic little laugh at that, but she didn't answer him.

Ben crossed his arms over his chest and leaned his back against the fence, looking off into the distance where darkness swallowed the trees. He could feel a tension in her. A sadness. But he didn't understand it. Since nothing else he said got a rise out of her, he tried something he knew would. "I have a confession."

"And I look like a priest?" she finally asked in a feeble attempt to be glib.

"I just gave your sister your car keys and sent her back to her husband."

Silence fell again for a moment. Ben waited for the explosion.

It didn't come. Instead she spoke with resignation. "I figured she went in to call Carl and make up."

"She thought you'd be mad," he said, testing the waters, thoroughly confused now.

Molly shook her head, her hair shifting loosely about her shoulders. "It's her life and her business." Then she sighed and looked down at the ground, pressing the top of her head to the fence. "Besides, I can understand it. Being around your family isn't easy."

"Funny, your sister alluded to the same thing. Why is that?"

Molly almost choked on another ironic laugh. "Don't sound offended. It isn't an insult. They're great people. I really like them. So does Karen. I think it just made us both seriously jealous."

"Jealous," Ben repeated. "I thought you didn't get jealous?"

Molly turned her face up to look at him, keeping her head to the fence. "Do you know how lucky you are? How lucky all of your family is?"

"Yes," he answered easily enough. "I'm not blind or stupid. We had a great childhood, great parents. In fact I was lying in bed thinking about it this morning and appreciating it."

She grimaced. "It's definitely something to appreciate."

Ben looked off into the trees again. After a while he sighed. "Since the day we met, a part of me has wanted to know what's going on with you, Molly. What happened with your dad, why you feel the way you seem to about him. And another part of me has wanted to avoid it like the plague. The more I get to know you, the more I realize whatever it is can't be good, and he was my friend. I guess the part of me that was John Northrup's friend doesn't want to know the bad."

"Then I won't tell it," she said defensively.

Now it was Ben who gave an ironic half laugh. "I told you last night that I love you, Molly. I meant that. I want to know everything about you, everything from your past, everything that bothers you, that drives you. If that tarnishes some of my conceptions about John Northrup, well, I'll live through it. Better that than letting it stay locked up inside you."

Silence again.

"Talk to me, Molly. Tell me your side, and then I'll tell you mine."

She waited so long to say anything that he wasn't sure she was going to. Then she jammed her hands into the front pockets of her jeans and turned around so that her back pressed into the fence the way Ben's did. "I don't know why, but tonight it's all on the surface."

"Good, then let's peel it away and get rid of it once and for all."

She hesitated for a moment, and Ben watched her shoulders hunch, as if she were curling into herself protectively. Just when he thought she had changed her mind about talking she began.

"He was a great father for a while," she admitted. "Until I was about nine he was terrific, just like a big, mischievous playmate. I guess it could be argued that that didn't make him a great father, but it seemed like it to me at the time. Whenever we were together, he turned everything into an adventure or a game—he was better at making up games than anyone I've ever known. He used to take me to play tennis every weekend...."

Her voice had turned wistful and then trailed off. Ben had the impression that she was remembering the good times. But then her tone hardened.

"He had an affair—I only learned later that it wasn't his first. He came home and announced that he just didn't want to be married any more. Simple as that. And without much more thought. Then he walked out." She sighed a short, harsh breath. "I always laugh when I hear that new cliché about how the parents are divorcing each other and not the kids. Whoever invented that wasn't a child of divorce, or at least of divorce the way I know it." She cleared her throat and went on more matter-of-factly. "When my father got divorced, he divorced us all. It was as if he had been interested in us for as long as we amused him. But once he tired of the role of husband and father, he dumped the three of us like old shoes. As if he were a kid trashing a toy he got bored with...."

She seemed to drift for a moment again. Ben didn't say anything. It wasn't easy for him to listen to this and yet it somehow fitted his image of John Northrup.

"He made big promises when he left," she said. "He wasn't really deserting us, I remember him saying. He knew the house and Karen and me were too much for Mama to take care of all by herself while she tried to make a living for the first time in her life. So he said he'd pay support money, mow the grass, come over if anything broke down or we needed him at any time, for any reason.... He was still going to be a part of our life. What a laugh. Those were the beginning of the empty promises. When my mother tried to get him to stick to his word, it was a different story. He was a busy man. He had a new life of his own. Karen and I would eavesdrop, and no matter what my mother said or did, she couldn't get him to keep his word. I guess I saw her frustration with him before I started to experience it myself."

Ben heard her swallow. When she went on, her voice was little more than an emotion-clogged whisper.

"Kids always know so much more than their parents think they do. We saw how afraid Mama was when he wouldn't pay the support. We knew how frustrated she was every time he pulled the rug out from under her by reneging on his promises. But we pretended we didn't know how upset she was. She tried to protect us. We tried to protect her.'' Molly gave a bitter laugh. "And my father didn't think about protecting anyone but himself. Certainly protecting Karen and me was the last thing on his mind.''

Molly tipped her head back and looked up at the stars. "He was a perpetual child who never thought about anyone but himself. After the divorce when I would see him without my mother I'd always feel strange, as if I were more the adult. He seemed to expect me to console him, to concede to anything he wanted, to excuse him. He'd flaunt his girlfriends as if we should be impressed—this one's a model, that one's an airline stewardess, this one's God's gift to mortal man. He'd tell us about his parties and ski trips and vacations and expensive wining and dining— without ever once thinking that at the same time Karen and I were going to junior high wearing our mother's hand-me-downs because we couldn't afford the kinds of clothes other kids had, that we couldn't go to the movies with our friends because there was no money, that we were having to sell our house, leave our friends and live off the charity of my grandparents because my mother couldn't earn enough for us to live and he only paid support money when he felt like it. God.'' Molly breathed a disgusted sigh before continuing angrily.

"He'd always follow up his stories with big promises. What he was going to buy us, provide for us, where he was going to take us, what he was going to teach us. How much he loved us...

"And he was so damn charming and so damn convincing when he was making his promises to us that we overlooked most of his bragging and just hung on to that part of his exciting, fun life that he was going to let us have a little piece of. But his words to us were as empty as they had been to my mother. He talked a good game, but it never happened. Not once did he refuse himself a single second of his partying to be with us. He never once altered a plan, never once followed through with a promise, never once made us a priority in his life. He was his priority."

Ben watched her as she took her hands out of her pockets, hugged her own middle and bent over at the waist to bob up and down a few times as if she was too agitated to stand still.

"I can still remember the sound of Karen's voice begging him. I decided early on that he'd never see how much he hurt me, but Karen..."

She stopped bobbing and stood up straight. To Ben it looked like the same kind of pride that she must have found in herself then, that pride that wouldn't allow her to beg the way her sister had.

"Right after giving us a big speech about how much he wanted to see more of us, he'd call and say he wasn't even going to make it for the few hours he usually saw us because he was just too busy with his own life. Karen would plead in this pitiful please-love-me voice, swearing that she wanted to help him help his girlfriend move or sit in the park alone while he played tennis or help him keep score during his golf game or meet his girlfriend's parents, too. Sometimes I guess he'd feel guilty and give in. I never went with him then. No matter how much I was missing him. And I'd get so mad listening to her plead. 'But you promised...'

"By the time he left for California, I was half glad that he was going. I knew better than to believe everything he said about bringing Karen and me out there when he got settled, about spending our summers with him. I figured at least they would be the last of the empty promises. I was right. We never heard from him again. Not even when my mother had a stroke and died six months later."

"Good God, Molly," Ben said compassionately. "Not even then?"

She turned back to face the tennis courts. "Probably *especially* not then. He might have had to take up being a father again and raise us. But it was okay," she said in a way that told him that nothing about it was okay. "After we lost the house, we had gone to live with my grandparents, anyway. Thank God we had them."

Her voice grew stronger, determined. "My grandmother raised us. She was a gem. We had my grandfather to give us hugs and kisses and compliments and reason with us when we thought we were being unfairly treated. My uncle roughhoused with us and fixed our bikes and lit our fireworks, his wife took us for a special new skirt or blouse to start school in. My great-aunt and -uncle would take us to the movies or amusement parks, the expensive entertainments that were special treats."

She had to stop for a minute. The determination in her voice gave way to something else. When he realized she was fighting tears, it nearly ripped him apart. He turned and put his arms around her. She didn't push him away, but she was stiff and proud and unyielding, forcing herself to finish what she was saying.

"It wasn't as if we were denied a lot after that. And I was always grateful and happy that someone loved me enough to do it, to go to the trouble or the expense. But I also always felt like a charity case. And I always knew it wasn't the way it should have been, that my family wasn't what it should have been. All the while my father was off providing for himself, entertaining himself, thinking about himself, absorbed in himself...."

Ben just held her for a while, even though she didn't respond. He didn't feel rejected—he knew she was just lost in the pain of her past. How to soothe that pain was something he wasn't sure about. But as he stood there picturing the man he had known in the context in which Molly had just put him, he began to see much of what he knew of John Northrup in a different perspective.

Ben turned his head and laid it on top of hers. "I don't know if it helps or not, Molly, but it really wasn't anything wrong with you or Karen or your mother. It probably seems strange, but I think you were just the first victims of whatever made John tick. Or maybe I should say whatever made John run. He couldn't stick to anything. I always just accepted that in him. It didn't do me any harm, so I took it as a quirk he had."

He felt her stiffen and went on to explain. "I saw him go from one woman to another, but from where I stood, that just made him look like a lady's man. I saw him go from one obsessive interest to another without a backward glance at what had lost his attention, but since it usually took the form of a new sport—nothing really important—it didn't strike me as a serious character flaw. In fact, his short attention span seemed like energy and vibrancy. I see now that the flip side of the coin was that he had been as fickle in his commitment to you."

He felt some of her tension ease. She turned her head and let him pull her close to his body.

"Strange," Ben went on, encouraged to feel her relaxing, "but I used to think that he was seriously claustrophobic—not so much in terms of closed spaces, but in his own head. It was as if committing himself to anything made him feel trapped, triggering the phobia, and he had to get himself out at any expense. But until tonight it didn't occur to me that at one time it had cost him you. I hurt for you, but believe me, Molly, he paid the greater price."

When she finally put her arms around him, he breathed a sigh of relief and held her tight. "I love you, Molly," he said into her hair.

She didn't answer him, but he hadn't expected her to. Enough had been said between them, and he sensed her need for silence now. So he just stayed holding her for a long, long time.

When all the sounds from the patio had died, Ben took her back up to the house. But rather than walk her to her bedroom, he guided her into the living room. First he turned on the television, and then he went to one of the flowered sofas.

"I can't leave you tonight." He lay on the couch and reached his arms up for her. "So here we are, just two people who innocently fell asleep watching TV."

Molly smiled down at him. "You're a nice man, Boyd," she said softly, and lay beside him.

He closed his arms around her, holding her against his body. "Now go to sleep before I forget I'm in my parents' home," he whispered into her hair.

She did just that, apparently exhausted.

But for Ben it wasn't so easy. He couldn't get out of his mind the thought that for the first time he had really seen just how vulnerable Molly was.

And more than that, just how scared to believe in any man.

Chapter Nine

Molly woke to him rubbing her back.

"So tell me," Ben whispered huskily into her hair. "Have you ever gone skinny-dipping at dawn in a stream-fed pond?"

At first, Molly wasn't sure where she was. She knew she was in Ben's arms, but that was about it. And in that semiconscious state—held close to him, breathing in the scent that was his alone, feeling his body around hers—it didn't matter that no other thought intruded.

"Never," she whispered back thickly.

"I've been lying here thinking about what makes it a little too disrespectful for me to make love to you under my parents' roof. I haven't figured it out—must be something Freudian—but it did occur to me that the pond is sort of a no-man's land, and that makes it free ground. What do you say we stake a claim to it?"

All the while he was talking, he kept rubbing her back and her arm and then her side, down to her waist and way up to the outer swell of her breast. In that moment Molly learned something. Her body, warm and soft, was very, very responsive. "Mmm," she agreed languidly, "but do I have to swim first?"

That made him chuckle, setting off a rumble in his chest beneath her ear. "It was really only an excuse to get your clothes off."

For another moment they stayed as they were, melded together the way they had slept the night. In no hurry, Ben kept on rubbing her side, the tips of his fingers brushing much closer to the very edge of her nipple.

Then he pushed them both upright and from behind nuzzled the spot where her neck dipped into her shoulder as both of his palms slid down her arms all the way to her wrists and back again. Molly heard him take a deep breath and felt him sigh as if he were the most contented man on earth. It made her smile lazily, but it didn't make her open her eyes. The dreamlike quality was too nice to relinquish.

Her eyes stayed closed as he stood up, took her hand and pulled her to her feet, too, only opening when he began to tow her through the living room. But even then, wanting to maintain this feeling of total sensuality, she left her eyes opened to only tiny slits, just enough to avoid crashing into something.

With Ben leading the way, they slipped out the sliding doors onto the back patio, across the dew-moistened lawn, past the pool where he swept up two of the bath sheets folded on a table near the cabana, and on across the side of the mountain. The pond was totally surrounded by pine trees and shrubs, blocking it from view and leaving it shaded from the brilliance of the sunrise that dusted the eastern horizon.

Within the seclusion of the trees, Molly shivered slightly at the difference in temperature. Feeling it, Ben let go of her hand, put his free arm around her and pulled her in close to him for a moment before he spread the towels on the ground. Then he pressed her down on them and stretched out beside her, over her. The warmth returned with his body, and the languor that the cooler air had threatened stayed on. She closed her eyes again and sighed in the same contented way he had before.

Then his mouth covered hers. Molly welcomed his kiss. It was sweet and warm and wonderful. She parted her lips to match his and met his tongue as it came inside. Her desire was still slow, but rich and full within her. She savored the velvety feel of the inside of his mouth, the slippery warmth of his tongue against hers. Even the rough stubble of his morning beard was arousing.

He slid her T-shirt up and only paused in his kiss long enough to slip it over her head. Her bra disappeared, and then his hand replaced it, big and strong and firm and far preferable. And when the firm pressure of his kneading turned into the gentle pinch and roll of her nipple between his two fingers, it sent shock waves all the way through her, ending in the awakening of the very core of her and rousing a low, throaty moan.

Molly skimmed her hands up the back of his shirt, reveling in the hardness of his broad shoulders before she pulled it off over his head. Ben's mouth left hers for the second time to accommodate her undressing of him. He reached to tug the snap and zipper of her jeans free and then eased them down with the silky bit of panty she wore. Suddenly in much more of a hurry, he shed his own shorts swiftly and then came back to her, his naked body an exhilarating sensation of warm flesh and cool morning air.

This time when his mouth came to her, it was on her breast, first on the side and then at her nipple. Hard and aroused, he took the crest into his mouth, sucking, nipping, tracing the sensitive outer circle with his tongue, drawing it deeply and then just barely closing his lips around it, letting it chill dry while he kissed her belly and then lower.

She really could have been dreaming, so lost in sensation was Molly. It was a dream she never wanted to wake up from. Every nerve in her body was alive with the most gloriously patient desire. She explored him with her hands, with her mouth. She discovered the hardness of his own aroused nipples with her tongue, while her hand found that other hardness and learned that her slightest touch orchestrated a frenzy in him.

And then he covered her body completely with his own, nudged her knees apart and found his place between her thighs. Slowly, tenderly, tentatively, he penetrated just the slightest bit into her and then retreated. Then just a little deeper and out again. And again. Until Molly wanted him so badly that she slid her hands down from his shoulders to the valley of his back and then lower, trying not to let him leave her again by clasping the tight mounds of his derriere.

Through the merger of agony and ecstasy within her, she heard him chuckle just before he obliged and pressed fully, completely, deeply within her. By then Molly was ready to explode with need for him. Each thrust told her his own need was every bit as intense, until first she and then he shed all languor and burst into a climax made all the stronger by the power in its slow, steady build.

And then Ben circled her with his arms and dropped his face to the side of her neck. "I love you, Molly," he murmured heavily.

"I love you, too." The words escaped before she had thought about it, a reflex as instinctive as her response to him. It jolted her out of her reverie.

Maybe he hadn't heard....

But he sighed once more, a sound of complete satisfaction that she knew ran much deeper than physical satiety. Then he laughed that full, rich, deep laugh of his and rolled to his back, his arms spread in a parody of joyful thanksgiving. "Finally," he said with extreme exaggeration and then expounded melodramatically. "And the sun broke through the treetops in rays of glory, and trumpets heralded from heaven."

"Wise guy," Molly muttered a little shakily.

He looked over at her out of the corners of his eyes and raised his unruly eyebrows. "Oh, yeah, and the earth shook," he finished smugly.

"Maybe for you," she deadpanned.

"For you, too, you little nymphette. You can't fool me."

"Egomaniac."

He rolled on top of her again, smiling down at her. "Say it again."

"Egomaniac," she complied, purposely obtuse.

"You know what I mean. Say you love me again."

"Egomaniac," she responded instead, intensely uncomfortable.

His teasing expression changed, and for a moment he stared down into her face. Then he smiled and said confidentially, "I've got your number, Molly Mercer."

Molly suddenly felt very serious. "Then you're one up on me, because even I don't have it."

He nuzzled her ear and then whispered into it. "Just ride with the feelings and let the rest of it go."

She'd already done that. But the ride was too fast and much, much too treacherous. She should have known better.

Gently but firmly she pushed him away and sat up, quickly pulling on her clothes. "I *did*," she said with finality. "And now it's back to business as usual."

He didn't answer her immediately, but she could feel him watching her. A quick glance told her he was frowning over at her, all teasing, all levity gone. "This isn't the end," he said as she nearly jumped to her feet and yanked one of the towels up after her just to give herself something to do.

"Yes, it is," she told him bluntly. "It's the end of my binge."

And then she nearly ran back to the house.

"I want you to buy me out of your restaurants," Molly announced not half a mile away from the Boyds' house on their way home that afternoon.

It was the first thing she had said directly to Ben since leaving him at the pond that morning. The large Boyd clan had made that easy—she had just mingled with them. But all the while she did, she had felt such panic. Such a need to run. It wasn't rational. It probably wasn't even sane.

Now, alone with Ben in his car, she knew what she had to do.

"No, I won't buy you out," Ben said flatly, glancing back over his shoulder as he merged onto the highway.

"Look..." Molly tried to sound reasonable. "We've had a nice little fling..."

"I thought it was a binge."

"Whatever." Molly waved it away and went on. "But it's time to get down to business. In the long run you'll be better off without partners to interfere or take a cut of your profits, and Karen and I will be better off with Mercer Moving and Storage."

"What's your insurance going to do about that wrecked truck?" he challenged, his eyes on the road.

"I wish you'd slow down a little," she said instead. "The accident just happened Friday night. You know I haven't had a chance to find that out. And that's not what we're talking about."

"Take a guess, Molly," he persisted. "You must have some idea."

Her attempt to remain reasonable and businesslike was being tested by his obvious anger. Her tone took on a heated edge. "I don't know."

"Don't you? Well, it's been my experience that you never come out of an accident without paying something. As a rule, the older the vehicle, the less the insurance considers it's worth and the more the expense to you."

"I'll manage," she said, now watching the tail end of the van in front of them. "Besides, that has nothing to do with what we're discussing. Buy me out and the expense won't matter."

"Mercer Moving and Storage is dying. You'd be throwing good money after bad."

"You don't know what you're talking about," she shot back at him.

"Be sensible, Molly. You'll have a steady stream of money coming in from the restaurants. Mercer Moving and Storage is only a steady stream going out."

He began a sharp pass on the van, veering across the double yellow line that divided this narrow two lane section of the mountain highway.

"If you keep driving like this you'll kill us both and we won't have to worry about it."

"We?" he mocked. "Is there a we? Isn't that too threatening to you? I wouldn't think anyone came out of a *binge* as a *we*."

He passed not only the van, but a Honda, too, before swinging back into the lane. Molly was beginning to wonder if he was going to make it without hitting a pickup truck head-on. When he did, she let out the breath she had been holding. "We can come to a reasonable buy-out price and set up whatever terms you want."

"No," he repeated, and then followed it with a colorful obscenity as he glanced in his rearview mirror.

Molly looked back over her shoulder and found a state patrol car right behind them, red and blue lights flashing.

Serves you right, she thought, but said nothing. Ben pulled over onto the shoulder of the road and got out of the car as the patrolman stopped behind them and met him halfway. Molly just stayed where she was, tapping the knuckles of her fist against the seat.

How had she gotten into all this? she thought as she stared out her side window at the roadside. The binge had gotten out of hand. Like the flu, she had caught love. And she didn't want it.

Talking so much about her father last night had been a vivid reminder of things she didn't often think about anymore. It seemed like an omen to her. She had been letting her guard down, losing sight of what was so important for her to remember. Look at her mother. Look at Karen....

Ben got back in the car, crumpling the ticket and tossing it onto the dashboard. When he didn't start the engine, Molly glanced over at him. He was staring out his side window, his chin in the curve of his thumb and index finger, his expression dark, angry and thoughtful all at once. She decided to try reasoning with him again.

"I have to hold onto Mercer Moving and Storage," she told him solemnly. "Yes, I could go out and get another job, or I could sit back and just collect profitsharing from you or maybe I could force you to use me in your restaurants. But any of those would put me under someone else's control. Someone else would have the power over me, over my future, the power to make me or break me...."

"The same kind of power your father had over your mother," he put in bitterly.

Molly ignored the remark and continued. "I can't have that. I can't. I'd rather have the uncertainty of the slumps in my own business. I'd rather have all the responsibility, all the problems, because at least then I have control. I can work my tail off, cut back, do whatever it takes to make a go of it and not rely on anyone."

He turned his head slowly to look over at her, his steel-colored eyes shaded beneath a deep frown. "It's out of your control, anyway. Your company is going down regardless."

"I can revive it. I just need to liquidate my *inherit-ance*." The word sounded facetious even though she hadn't meant it to.

Ben shook his head. "I understand your determination to be independent, to avoid anyone having the kind of power over you that your father had over your mother, the kind that leaves you vulnerable to having your whole life destroyed at someone's whim. But the plain truth, Molly, is that I swore to your father that I would only buy you out if it was in your best interests, and never if the money was going into Mercer Moving and Storage. I'd be violating both those vows if I bought you out now."

Molly threw up her hands and shouted, "But now you know what kind of person he was! How can you refuse me in order to honor a promise to a man who never kept a promise or a vow or a commitment in his entire life?"

"Yes, he was a bastard to you and your mother!" he shouted back. "But this isn't John Northrup we're talking about. This is me. My word of honor. My integrity. My ethics. I made a promise to him. It doesn't matter what kind of person he was. It matters that I swore it."

"What terrific irony. I got burned because he couldn't stick to his word, and burned again because he extracted a promise from someone who could. That's a good one. The joke's on me either way."

"Funny, because it sure as hell feels like the joke's really on me," he muttered under his breath. Then he hooked his left wrist over the steering wheel, stretched his right arm along the back of the seat and leaned toward her, stabbing her with a narrow-eyed glare. "You know what I think, Molly? I think that you keep all your old wounds right there on the surface to remind you not to feel anything for a man. Whatever you do, don't take a risk—isn't that the idea? But something you hadn't planned happened. You met me. You fell in love with me. And now you want to run like hell. This whole issue of your inheritance is just a smoke screen you're using to hide behind while you make your escape.''

"You're mingling two separate issues," she protested too much, not looking at him.

"Am I?" he asked facetiously. "And if I were to buy you out today, when would I see you again?"

She only repeated, "They're separate issues. I want you to buy me out because I need the money. But whether you do or not, our relationship has gone too far too fast and it needs to have some serious skids put on it."

For a long moment Ben didn't say anything. Molly could feel his eyes boring into her profile. Then, very seriously, he said, "I think we're through."

Molly's throat constricted instantly. A part of her shouted for her to deny it. A stronger part just turned her head to look out her side window again.

A harsh, mirthless laugh came from Ben. "Bingo," he muttered bitterly, confirming his own words. Then he started the car, jammed it into gear and sped back onto the highway. "I'm going to do you two favors. I'm *not* going to buy you out of my restaurants, because then you'll at least have a living when that business of yours fails—"

"And you'll have a clear conscience," she cut him off snidely. "Although I'll never understand how keeping a promise to anyone like my father can give you that."

He went on without acknowledging her interruption. "And personally...I'm going to drop you off at your tidy little house, drive away and leave you the hell alone. Totally and completely. To go back into hiding."

Chapter Ten

Just getting out of bed was a chore. As a result Molly was late for work when she left the house a week later on Monday morning.

The six days since Labor Day had been a long and lonely week. And as she drove to Mercer Moving and Storage, Molly felt rotten.

Vitamins gave her headaches. Unsweetened cranberry juice tasted like battery acid. Lettuce did not satisfy and soothe the way chocolate did. Cough syrup tasted like fruit-flavored shoe polish. Aerobics made her sweat and pant, and jogging couldn't compare to sitting in an air-conditioned movie theater. It was a fact of life that everything that was good for you was not nice or fun or pleasant in any way.

It only followed that breaking it off with Ben—which she considered good for her—made her miserable. Anything else would be against the laws of nature.

She hadn't even had her sister to keep her company. Karen and the girls had not only moved out of her house, but Carl had taken them all on an impromptu vacation to celebrate the reconciliation. Nancy had been swamped with visiting in-laws and had even taken three days off work.

And Ben had done just what he said he was going to do. He had left her the hell alone.

It had been one of the worst weeks of her life, and as Molly pulled into Mercer Moving and Storage's parking lot, she was glad it was over and a new one was starting.

Most of the trucks were already out, and the warehouse crew was taking their morning break under the shade of an oak tree, some of them sitting at the picnic table Molly had put there, others lying on the grass. She waved when she got out of the car, but didn't go over to chat. She just wasn't up to chatting.

Instead she flung the door open just a little too forcefully—it slipped out of her hands and banged into the wall behind it. She grimaced at the resounding noise, ignored the stares she knew she was drawing and pulled the door closed behind her.

The sound of her flat heels on the cement warehouse floor drew Nancy's glance up from her work. The secretary's smile was wan. "I hope you managed to get at least a couple of hours of sleep last night," she said in greeting.

Molly had known Nancy long enough to tell by the look on her face that there was more behind that statement than concern. "I'm going to be sorry I got up at all today, aren't I?'' she guessed, and then went on fatalistically. "Now what?''

Her friend's smile was pained. "Are you sure you want to hear it right away?''

Heading into her office, Molly said over her shoulder, "I'm sure I don't want to hear it. Ever. But since there's no such luck, we might as well get it over with.''

She opened the bottom drawer of her desk and dropped her purse into it. Then she sank in her chair and rested her head against the back. She wasn't up to this. Actually, she wasn't up to anything.

By then Nancy had followed her and closed the office door—not a good sign.

"Okay, let's have it.''

"The good news or the bad news?''

Molly cracked a small smile. "Do good first.''

"Actually, I guess the good news is a couple of different parts of the same subject—the accident. Nothing in the truck wreckage shows anything mechanically faulty. The lawyer finally got hold of the report on Dick's blood alcohol level. It was twice the legal limit, the police are ticketing him for drunk driving and he has no grounds to sue. In fact the lawyer says you could sue him.''

"You can't get blood out of a turnip. The only thing suing the driver would accomplish is my having to pay legal fees on top of everything else.''

"On top of everything else is right.''

Molly grimaced. "I take it that was a warning for the bad news.''

Nancy nodded and passed Molly several sheets of paper. "The insurance coverage on the truck,'' she explained ominously.

Molly only looked at one thing—the amount for which the check was made out. Then she laughed a little hysterically. "This'll buy about half a truck."

"I know. I already called for an explanation. They said the truck was old and this was the blue book value—the most your policy requires that they cover."

For a moment Molly just stared at the check. The truck couldn't be repaired, and the insurance money didn't come anywhere near buying even a used replacement.

"Molly? Are you okay? You look kind of green."

She felt as if she were moving in slow motion as she lifted her head to look at Nancy. She tried to smile. "I'm fine. Is there more?"

Nancy frowned, hesitated and then said, "The Petrys' attorney called."

Molly had contacted Mrs. Petry about the damaged antiques on Friday. "Mrs. Petry seemed so understanding. She said she didn't think there would be a problem taking payments on what I couldn't pay up front. Why did they call in a lawyer?"

"Apparently a lot of the things were family heirlooms from *Mr.* Petry's side. He wasn't so understanding."

Molly shook her head. "Don't tell me—we've avoided a lawsuit from Dick, but now the Petrys are suing."

"No, not yet, but there was that underlying threat. What their lawyer says they want is their own people—his term—to assess the damages, and then they'll decide what they'll accept refinished—again, by their own people. As for replacements, they want to contact their own dealers to equal the quality and just send us the bills. You can make payments to the dealers and the refinishers, but not to the Petrys."

"They're due the value of what was lost, not a blank check to buy anything their little hearts desire." Then she laughed, again hysterically. "Well, the insurance money from the truck might cover the Petrys' claim and keep them from suing us."

Nancy didn't say anything.

"Of course then we'll be out another truck and down to a fleet of three, but . . ." Molly dropped her head onto her desk and groaned rather than finishing her sentence. "I think I need a double hot fudge banana split."

That made her friend laugh. "At ten in the morning?"

"It's all right. I already ate a package of chocolate chip cookies for breakfast."

"What are you going to do?" Nancy asked.

Without lifting her head off her desk, Molly shrugged. "Beats me."

Silence elapsed for a moment before Nancy asked, "*Has* it beaten you?"

Again Molly shrugged, but before she could answer, the phone rang. She didn't budge, so Nancy reached across the desk and picked it up.

"It's Karen," the secretary said after a brief conversation.

Molly didn't immediately respond to that, either. But finally she took a deep breath and slid into an upright position again to take the phone.

As Nancy headed out of the office, she whispered in an aside, "If you're serious about the double hot fudge banana split, I'll buy. Just let me know."

"Thanks," Molly said as the door closed behind her friend. Then she put the phone to her ear. "Hi," she said dispiritedly.

"You sound awful. Are you sick?"

"Just tired. How was your trip?"

"It was good. A little tense, but good."

"That's nice. How are you and the girls doing?"

Instead of answering, Karen repeated, "You really don't sound right, Molly. What's the matter?"

Molly had the distinct impression that her sister would rather not talk about what was going on at her house, so she answered Karen's question. "Well, let's see. Where shall I start?" she said facetiously. "There's Dick the drunk driver, lawyers, lawsuits, threatened lawsuits, rotten insurance coverage, an already limping fleet of trucks reduced from four to three when even four weren't enough, and less than understanding prima donna customers whose antiques weren't just antiques but were *heirlooms* that will require a pound of my flesh before we can call things square. But that's about it."

"And you haven't heard from Ben all week, have you?"

Molly rolled her eyes and snapped, "Of course not. I told you before that we were finished. Why would I have heard from him? And it doesn't matter. God knows I have so many problems I wouldn't have time to think about him even if I wanted to, which I don't."

Only in the silence that followed did Molly realize how loud her voice had been. "I'm sorry. I didn't mean to shout at you."

"Did it ever occur to you that if you weren't on the outs with Ben, you could deal with the other problems better?"

"No, it didn't."

"Don't bite my head off. I'm just trying to help. Whether you want to admit it or not, you're upset about Ben. Knowing you, you've been on a chocolate bender for the past week, haven't you?"

"No."

"Have you gotten to double hot fudge banana splits yet?"

"No."

Karen half sighed, half laughed. "Why don't you just give in, Molly?"

It was on the tip of Molly's tongue to really let her sister have it. What should she give in to? Being vulnerable to a man the way Karen had? The way her mother had? So she could be cheated on, used, controlled, manipulated and ultimately dumped when the grass looked greener? But all she said was, "No, thanks."

This time Karen's sigh sounded defeated. "I have to go in to Boyd's sometime today to tell Ben I won't be working for him anymore. Want me to tell him something for you?"

"Are you sure you should quit?" Molly asked instead.

"Carl doesn't like the idea of my working."

Molly bit back a comment about why it shouldn't matter what Carl did or didn't like. Then a thought occurred to her. "There is something you could talk to Ben about."

"Anything." Karen sounded hopeful.

"See if you can convince him to buy us out."

Again there was silence on the line. Molly decided she was getting really tired of the disapproval all these silences were conveying.

"Karen? Did you hear me?"

"I heard you."

When she didn't say any more, Molly snapped again, "I suppose Carl doesn't like the idea of that, either?"

"Carl doesn't have anything to do with that. I'm just not sure it's the wisest thing. Maybe Ben is right and we're better off with his profit-sharing."

Molly fumed, but hid her anger behind forced patience. "Okay. Then why don't you see if you can convince him to buy *me* out?"

"Don't be like this, Molly."

Molly took a deep breath and tried hard to remain calm. "I want out of Boyd's Restaurants. Mercer Moving and Storage is going to die if I don't come up with some money to pump into it. That's the bottom line."

"What about Ben?"

"What about Ben?" Molly nearly shrieked.

"Personally."

"I told you, that's over."

"But it shouldn't be."

Now it was Molly's turn to sigh. "Look, I know you're on some kind of romantic high, Karen, and I'm glad for you. But everything between Ben and me is over. Finished. *Finis. Finito.* And that's how I want it. I'm glad." Her stomach lurched, and her heart was in her throat.

Another one of those disapproving silences fell before Karen said dubiously, "Okay. If you say so. If you really think it's the best business move, I'll talk to him."

"Great," Molly choked out. Then she swallowed and tried to force her voice to sound normal. "I definitely think it's the best business move. Independence is always the best way."

"Even now?" Karen ventured in a tone that was barely audible.

Molly ignored it. "So you will try to convince him?"

"I'll try."

"Then call me the minute you get home and let me know what he has to say. About buying us out," she suddenly felt the necessity to add.

"I'll call you as soon as I get back, but it won't be until later today."

"That's okay. Talk to you then." Molly hung up and sat back in her chair, feeling much better. She wasn't beaten. Mercer Moving and Storage would make it yet.

"I'd be real careful if I were you. There's a thorn in the lion's paw."

Ben heard the comment his chef made just outside his office door. Temperamental damn cooks, he thought. This wasn't the first time he'd rejected an experimental recipe, so what was the big deal?

"What now?" he demanded in answer to the knock on his open door a few moments later. Then he looked up from his paperwork to find Karen Dune standing there, obviously unsure of herself. He tried to smile and sound more friendly. "Karen. I didn't expect you. Come in."

She still looked wary, but she did as he'd said, sitting in the chair across from the walnut table that served as his desk.

"How was your trip?" Ben asked, trying to put her more at ease.

"Nice," she said. "I loved Disneyland as much as the girls did. I'm sorry about leaving a message on your machine that I wouldn't be in last week. But we decided on the spur of the moment, and I couldn't get hold of you. . . ." Her voice trailed off.

"That's okay. I understood. Ready to go back to work?" Ben watched her face color at that. But before she had a chance to answer him, the chef's assistant knocked on the still-open door.

"What?" he snapped out so loudly that both Karen and the young cook jumped.

"The produce delivery truck just pulled up. You said you wanted to talk to them," the assistant said rapidly.

"Get Janet to do it. I pay her to be the manager, let her do some managing. She knows what the problem is. And close that damn door."

This time when he looked back at Karen, she was suppressing a smile. "You're in as bad a mood as Molly is, aren't you?"

Ben laughed a little ruefully at that and rocked back in his chair. "Me? In a bad mood? Nah."

"Sorry, don't know what could have made me think it."

His mood in the past week had been discussed and commented on more than he could stand, so rather than get into it, Ben guessed about why Karen was here. "You came to quit, didn't you?"

That subdued her amusement. "Carl doesn't want me to work," she said simply.

He shrugged. "I half expected it."

"I'm sorry."

"Don't be. It's no problem." He wanted to ask about Molly, but he swallowed the words. Instead he said, "How are things on the home front?"

Karen shrugged. "All right. It's kind of strange, while you're separated, your problems are an open book, and the more people who know and sympathize with you, the better you feel. Then things go back to the way they were before, the problems turn private again, and it's embarrassing that everybody knows so much about what went on."

"I guess that makes sense." It also told him the subject was taboo. "So, how is Molly?" The words came out on their own when he couldn't think of anything else to say.

"Crabby. I need to talk to you about that."

"About Molly being crabby?"

"No, about the inheritance."

That dropped like a rock. "Uh-huh . . ." was all he said.

"I really do think it would be best if you bought us out, Ben," she began. "I know there are a lot of good arguments against it. I've made some myself. But in the end I have to agree with Molly that we're better off in control of things. That will never happen unless we maintain ownership of Mercer Moving and Storage, and to do that we need a little capital put back into it."

Ben watched her intently. "I promised your father that I wouldn't do that."

"I know you did. Molly told me all about it. But my father didn't really have any idea what was best for Molly and me or what our situation is. I think there has to be flexibility. I guess in a way it's like getting married and swearing that you'll never hurt each other. Things happen, things change, people get hurt anyway and learn they have to roll with the punches."

"I don't agree. I think vows should be kept so there aren't any punches to roll with."

She paled at that, and Ben regretted his words. He really was in a foul mood. "I'm sorry. That was out of line."

She went on as if he had never said anything. "Try to understand, Ben. Our father waved a lot of carrots in front of our noses only to yank them away just when we needed them most. It was very cruel. The terms of this inheritance seem like history repeating itself."

"I gave my word, Karen," he said stubbornly. "That means something to me."

"Just think about it," she urged as she stood to go. She walked to the door before turning back to him. "I really do appreciate your hiring me."

He waved it away. "Sure. No big deal. You are my partner, after all."

"Not for long, I hope." She hesitated in the doorway before turning back and venturing tentatively, "I also think giving in on this might smooth the waters with Molly."

"Did she say that?"

"No. It just seems to me that if she has that security bolstering her she might give in and risk a little on the personal front. Just think about it," she repeated.

As if he could think about anything but a way to make Molly give in and take a risk on him. But Ben forced a smile at Karen. "You have to practice sounding more convinced yourself before you can get anybody to believe you."

Karen shrugged. "Isn't it worth a try?" she asked, and then before he could say anything else, she was gone.

For a few minutes Ben stared after her, not really seeing anything at all. Then he went back to his paperwork. He added the same short column of numbers three times and lost track without managing to get a total. The figures on the invoices swam together. They just didn't make any sense. But then nothing made any sense lately.

When he failed to get the sum on the fourth try and then jammed the buttons on his pocket calculator by punching them too hard, he yanked his desk drawer open, slid the papers inside and slammed it closed again. Then he bounded up from his chair and out of this office.

"Tell Janet I'll be out for a while," he growled at his chef, and stormed through the back door.

It was past five, so people from the office buildings across the parking lot were beginning to get into cars to go home or wander over to Boyd's or Marie Callendar's for drinks or dinner. Ben dodged them and went into the first black-glass tower building he came to. Three women were getting off the elevator and the third held it for him, smiling as she did. He muttered a thanks and jabbed the number four button without returning her smile.

Rick's secretary was waiting in the corridor when the elevator doors opened on the fourth floor.

"Is he still in there?" Ben asked her, nodding to his brother's office just across the hall.

"You're in luck," the young brunette answered him as she replaced him in the elevator.

Ben didn't announce himself as he went in. He didn't make a sound until he got to Rick's inner office door. Then he leaned one shoulder against the jamb and said, "Boo."

Rick jerked around from an open filing cabinet drawer. Then realizing it was Ben, he said, "Damn you, you scared me to death."

Ben smiled. "Got a minute?"

"Yeah, as a matter of fact I do. I was going to stop over and bum a meal off of you. Tammi's taking the kids to a birthday party tonight, and I'm a free man."

Ben didn't comment. He pushed off the jamb and slouched down into one of the black leather chairs.

Rick shut the file drawer and came to sit on the sofa across from him. "I wondered if you were in a better mood. Guess I don't have to ask."

"What I am is sick of hearing about my mood," Ben groused. "I need a sounding board."

"That's what big brothers are for." Rick stretched his arms out along the back of the couch and seemed to settle in. "But as I recall, on Friday night when you told me about the promise you'd made to John, you didn't want to know what I thought."

"Well, now I do. I'm beginning to think Molly's a no-win situation and maybe you can see a different side to it."

"Okay. I can be an objective third party. Lay it on me and see if I can give you a different perspective. But be advised it's going to cost you the biggest lobster tail you've got when we're finished."

"Yeah, yeah," Ben agreed peevishly. Then he frowned at the discarded legal pad on the coffee table. "In a nutshell—if I keep my promise to John I can say here I am, a guy who sticks to his word, not the kind of man your father was, so you can trust me. But then that means I don't buy her out, she doesn't have the money to pump back into her own business, it'll die, she'll blame me, resent me, hate me, and I'll never get her to come around. But if I buy her out and give her what she wants, it just proves she was right, that she can't trust any man to keep his promises and she still won't have anything to do with me.''

Rick scratched his forehead. "Yeah, that fits my definition of a no-win situation, all right." After a moment's hesitation he said, "Let's just talk legalities. John Northrup is gone, and the only legally binding document he left behind was a will giving his daughters his share in your restaurants. The promise was verbal, and he's not around to hold you to it.''

"Now tell me something I don't know. I came over here for a different perspective, remember?''

"How about that he died and left you daddy?''

Ben looked up at his brother. That was definitely a different perspective.

"The way I read it," Rick continued, "there are a couple of things going on here that you can't see because you're in the middle of it. In a way John Northrup died and left you his kids and his dirty work. He didn't do a damn thing for Molly and Karen when he should have, and then when it was too late to infringe on his own time or life or pleasure or whatever, he made a big gesture to atone. Personally, I think that's too little too late.''

Ben shook his head in disgust. "I'm almost as sick of feeling defensive for John as I am of hearing about my bad mood. Okay, you think he was a creep, too. But I'm not responsible for that.''

"My second point—your intense sense of responsibility," Rick said smugly. "There's no way John could have known you as well as he did and not know how responsible you are. I think he just decided to use that for his own purposes. So he elected you dad and left you with orders for how to perform that job to take care of his kids over the long haul—don't buy them out, just support them with profit-sharing. That's pretty ludicrous when he didn't seem to worry about them being taken care of when they really needed him to. It's also a damned unfair position to put you in even if you hadn't fallen in love with Molly."

Ben stared out the window behind his brother's head. "Advice?" he asked, knowing he sounded angry.

"Give Molly what she wants. Her father's sins were his own. It's not your responsibility now to either make up for them or to take over parental support of two grown women."

"So I break my promise," Ben said more to himself than to Rick.

"I know the guy was your friend, but he wasn't square with you on this. Extract a promise under false pretense—which I consider this to be—and it isn't binding. Not legally, not morally, not ethically."

For a while Ben didn't speak. Rick's perspective made sense, but he hated to admit it. It made it seem as though John had used him.

Furthermore, Ben's feelings for Molly were anything but paternal. "Do you mind eating alone?" he said finally to his brother.

"Ordinarily I'd say yes, but tonight I don't think you'd be good enough company to make a difference."

"You're right." Ben took a deep breath and sighed. "I need a drive to clear some cobwebs, and then I think I have to go see a certain lady."

"Does this mean big brother did good or bad?"

Ben pushed himself out of the chair. "That remains to be seen."

"Pour on the charm," Rick advised as Ben headed for the door. "And let me know what happens."

Chapter Eleven

When the doorbell rang at eight that night Molly was sure it was Karen. Her sister had left a message on the answering machine that she would be by this evening to pick up the things the kids had left behind.

"Just a minute," she called, quickly grabbing up all the evidence of the double hot fudge banana split she had just polished off, disposing of it in the kitchen trash so Karen wouldn't see it and know just how depressed she was. Then she jogged back to the front door, saying as she opened it, "I didn't think I had locked the screen."

But it wasn't Karen standing on the porch.

It was Ben.

Molly went cold, then hot, then cold again. Her heart was in her throat, and her stomach suddenly rebelled against three double hot fudge banana splits consumed in one day. "Oh" was all she could say for a moment.

A single week had passed since she had seen him last, and yet it was like feasting her eyes on him for the first time in years. She had forgotten just how attractive he was. She had forgotten that just the sight of him made her skin sizzle. She had forgotten that she had been mad at him the last time they were together.

What she hadn't forgotten was that she loved him.

"I was expecting Karen," she said after trying to swallow back her response.

He just nodded. He seemed tired. "Can I come in?"

No, she wanted to say. But instead she shrugged as if she had no feelings one way or the other and opened the screen.

It was hard not to look at the breadth of his shoulders as she followed him from the entranceway into the living room. Harder still not to look at the tight curve of his derriere.

"I didn't mean to interrupt your dinner," he said as he glanced at the coffee table on his way to stand at the mantel. It wasn't until then that Molly remembered the open wrapper that held a hamburger with a single bite taken out of it, French fries she hadn't even tasted and a glop of unused ketchup.

"It's all right. It didn't taste good, anyway." She hurriedly wadded the wrapper around the uneaten food as if he'd be able to tell just by looking that she had taken one bite and then opted for The Diet of the Depressed instead. "Did you talk to Karen?" she asked as she went to throw the mess in the kitchen trash, having every intention of sticking strictly to business.

"She was in around five to quit," he called to her.

It unnerved her to look at him when she came back into the room, so instead Molly picked up the wooden apple that decorated the end table and dusted it against her jeans-clad leg. Then she realized what a rotten housekeeper that made her look like, replaced it and turned to fluffing the throw pillows on the end of the sofa.

"How have you been?" he asked after a few minutes.

"Fine," Molly snapped out too quickly, too desperately. "How have you been?"

"Miserable."

That made her feel better. It even gave her the courage to glance over at him as she straightened the magazines in the rack underneath the end table. "Is business bad?" she asked, purposely being obtuse.

"Business is great."

"Good."

Silence fell again.

Molly decided to take the bull by the horns. "Did Karen discuss the buy-out with you?"

That made him sigh in a way that sounded perturbed. "She did. She said it was what she wanted, too."

"And?" Molly prompted when he didn't go on.

"And I've thought about it."

"And?" she said a little more impatiently.

He pushed off the mantel and came toward her.

Molly's heartbeat did double time. She didn't move away from him—out of curiosity, she told herself.

Ben took her hand and pulled her to sit on the couch while he sat on the coffee table directly in front of her, his khaki-clad thighs straddling hers. He held both her hands lightly in his, watching his thumbs rub the smooth skin.

Molly swallowed with difficulty and told herself she was only cooperating so he'd buy her out of his business, not because it felt good.

"I've been feeling torn between you and your father," he said out of the blue, obviously by way of a beginning.

"I guess that makes sense," she answered, irked with herself for the softness in her voice. Business. Just business.

"He was my friend, Molly," Ben went on in a tone that asked her to acknowledge that. "I liked him. No, I don't like what he did to you. In fact I'm not too crazy about what I'm just beginning to realize he did to me. But there were things about him that were good and things that I got out of knowing him that were really beneficial to me. And within the context of a relationship that I valued, I made him a promise."

She could see his turmoil in the deep lines of his face. She didn't say anything. Apparently he hadn't expected her to, because he went on, anyway.

"But now it looks like his motives were purely selfish."

"Remember that he wasn't capable of anything else," she said snidely.

But Ben continued as if she hadn't spoken. "Rick said some things to me today that made a lot of sense. More sense than anything else I believed were your father's motives. I'm beginning to believe that the same way John passed off his responsibilities as a father onto your mother and your grandparents, he was trying to pass them off to me when he died."

Molly had to think about that for a moment. It was not something that had occurred to her. And yet the more she thought about it, the more in character it seemed.

If that was true, then what had looked like a means of her father controlling her, could actually have been regret for what he had done, as if in his own inept way he had tried to make up for it.

She choked out a grim laugh. "Strange."

"What is?"

She shook her head. "To think that as much as he was capable, he might have cared about us. At least enough to feel guilty. I guess that's something." Her eyes burned, and she closed them for a moment to cool them.

When she opened them it was to a deep, dark, troubled frown on Ben's face. "Why do you look like that? As if it makes you mad?"

He shook his head a little disgustedly. "It doesn't have anything to do with you. If this makes you see him a little less harshly, I'm glad. But in the same way it changes the way you see him, it alters my vision of some things, too."

"Obviously not favorably."

"I don't suppose it's logical, but I feel like he suckered me. Like he took my belief system and used it for his own benefit. Had I known the circumstances... Maybe it's splitting hairs, but it's one thing to do a favor for a friend, and another to do his penance for him." He paused before saying reluctantly, "Rick contends that a promise extracted with some secret agenda behind it is invalid."

Molly heard a note of question in that statement, as if Ben both agreed and disagreed with it. "And what do you think?" she asked carefully.

Ben didn't say anything at all for a few minutes. His thumbs still rubbed her hands, over and over again in warm circles. When he spoke, he didn't answer her question. "I've come with two choices for you." Frowning so fiercely that his brow was beetled, he spoke unenthusiastically. "If it's what you really want, I'll buy you and Karen out."

For a moment Molly wondered why it didn't make her feel any better. She should be glad for the end it meant in her connection with Ben. But all she could bring herself to say was "You said two choices."

He looked up into her eyes. His expression was very serious, his voice low and sincere. "The other one is that you don't accept the offer, that you let Mercer Moving and Storage die a natural death, take an active role in the restaurants . . . and marry me."

Surprise knocked the wind out of her sails. She didn't know what she had expected, but it wasn't a marriage proposal.

She suddenly couldn't sit still. The heat of his touch sluicing up her arms was too dangerous. Molly stood in a rush and charged to the mantel to straighten a candlestick there. "Boy, you'll really go all out not to have to break a promise, won't you? Even an invalid one," she said flippantly because she didn't know what else to say.

"Right now this has nothing to do with what I promised your father," he said solemnly, almost gravely.

"No?"

"No. I want you to let go of Mercer Moving and Storage because it's going down and I don't want to see you go down with it. I want you to come to work at the restaurants because you're a partner, because you would be an asset, and because I know you need a hand in the business that supports you. And I want you to marry me because I love you. Period."

"I don't agree that Mercer Moving and Storage is going down," she said rather than address the last. "And I think I would be making a mistake to give up control of my own business for a small partnership in yours."

"A hundred percent of a dying business is less valuable than twenty percent of a thriving one," he pointed out.

Not thinking clearly, Molly swiped her hand across the mantel shelf and blew the residual dust off her fingers. "Once I bring it back to life it'll be a hundred percent of a thriving business."

There was silence again.

Molly bent over to polish a fingerprint off the glass fire screen with the sleeve of her chambray shirt.

Then Ben's deep voice broke the tense silence. "Okay. Then take the buy-out, use the money for Mercer Moving and Storage and marry me, anyway."

Her hands were suddenly cold.

"Did you hear me, Molly?" he asked when she didn't answer him.

She stopped short and straightened up from shining the fire screen. Her lips were suddenly dry. She ran her tongue around them, but it didn't help. She plunged her hands into the pockets of her jeans to make them warm. "I heard you," she told him finally.

"Then forget business. I don't give a damn what you do with the money if you really want me to buy you out. Pump it into Mercer Moving and Storage or use it to float balloons over the north Atlantic, for all I care. We can keep everything to do with business out of it from this minute on. But marry me, anyway."

It was so tempting. So tempting . . .

"I just don't think it would work," she said frantically.

"Why wouldn't it work? You love me, I love you—"

"That doesn't matter," she said, cutting him off. Molly swallowed and let her head drop far back to look up at the ceiling, fighting the sting in her eyes.

"Nothing else matters more," he told her in a low, heartfelt tone.

"A lot of things matter more," she nearly shrieked.

"What?"

"Work, security, safety, independence . . ."

"Bull!" Then he said gently, "We love each other, Molly."

"It doesn't make any difference." She spun around, not realizing she was so near the rocking chair that she hit it and knocked it into a frenzied sway. "It doesn't really mean anything because it doesn't stick around. Feelings change, they go away, and so do the people who have them. Work, having your own life, being self-reliant, are the only things that mean anything, the only things you can count on. And that's all I want." She felt as if she was cracking, crumbling into little pieces.

Ben's voice was angry. Standing on the other side of the rocking chair, his hands rested on his hips. "You know what I think, lady? I think you're just like your father."

"You're crazy," she sneered.

"Am I? Not by a long shot. Most people think of bailing out when things get rough. But not you Northrups. Every time things got good, he saw it as a trap, it triggered his fear of commitment, and he bolted. When things get good for you, it triggers your fear of being let down or abandoned or rejected, and you bolt. The reasons may be different, but the response is just the same."

He dropped his head forward, shook it and breathed a deep sigh. When he looked at her again, he seemed more in control. "It's not that I don't understand it, Molly. God knows you've had some hard lessons. I know what your father did left scars. I know having your fiancé get cold feet and call off your wedding only confirmed your distrust. But I'm not like either of those men. If you let them, those scars and that distrust will control your life the same way John's fear of commitment did his. And you'll end up alone and regretting it, just the way he did. Don't let that happen. Marry me and give us a chance."

She shook her head so fast that the movement was like a tremor. "I can't."

He stepped around the chair and took her by the shoulders. His hands were big and steadying. She felt put back together with just his touch. His steel-gray eyes warmed her, lured her to doubt her own long-held beliefs.

"Yes, you can. You can do anything you want to. Just let go of all that old baggage."

It sounded so easy. It even felt possible. Maybe it could work for them....

The phone rang.

Molly stepped out of Ben's grasp and answered it. A woman's quivery voice asked for him. It took only seconds for him to take the call and then come back to the living room.

But it was long enough.

"I have to go," he announced in a frustrated tone. "That was Paula Brazos. She's in labor and I have to get her to the hospital. But we aren't finished here, Molly. Know that."

Molly was behind the rocking chair again, this time gripping the back with white knuckles. She recognized that feeling she had had when he had grasped her shoulders, that feeling of hope, of belief that just maybe this time it could be true. She had felt just the same way with every promise her father had ever made.

The interruption of the phone call had brought her back to her senses. She seized the let down of his leaving to renew her determination to protect herself.

"No," she said firmly, nearly shouting. "We are definitely finished. I want the buy-out. And I don't want to see you again when it's over."

"You don't mean that."

He began to step around the rocking chair the same way he had before the phone call, but this time Molly kept it like a wall between them. "I do. I mean it. I don't want to be married to you or anyone else," she said so fiercely that her words echoed with the strength of the feelings behind them.

"Fine," Ben shot out angrily. Then he shook his head. "You're hiding, Molly, and it's too late. I meant what I said. I'll buy you and Karen out." He took a paper from his shirt pocket and tossed it onto the seat of the rocking chair between them. "According to my accountant, that's the breakdown of what your forty percent is worth. I'll put the wheels in motion as soon as I can to get you your money. Then you'll have your business, your financial control. Your independence. And you'll still have your feelings for me."

"But I won't have you to hurt them."

He looked as if she had hit him. He gave a rueful laugh.

And then he agreed.

"No, you won't, not if that's how you want it."

She stabbed the air with her chin. "That is definitely how I want it."

He threw up both of his hands in defeat. "Then that's what you'll get. I hope it makes you happy."

He spun around and left.

For a moment Molly stayed behind the rocker, clutching on to the back for support. A part of her wanted to run after him, stop him, tell him she didn't mean anything she had said.

But years of reinforcement had made her distrust stronger.

"For crying out loud, I've been ringing the doorbell for ten minutes," Karen complained when Molly finally answered the door an hour later. As she came into the house she took a closer look at her sister. "Geez, you look awful."

"Thanks," Molly deadpanned, and led the way into the kitchen. "I was about to have a glass of iced tea. Want one?"

"Are you okay?" Karen asked rather than answer as she slung her purse over the back of a kitchen chair.

"Swell. How are things going with you?"

"All right. Tense, strange, but all right. We have an appointment with a marriage counselor tomorrow." Karen took the glass of iced tea that Molly brought her even though she hadn't said she wanted it and set at the table. "Looks to me like there's trouble right here in River City."

"Ben just left a little while ago."

"Well, you're pale as a ghost, so it couldn't have gone too well. Is he buying us out?"

"Yes." Molly slid her index finger up the side of her glass, not looking at her sister. She explained the reasoning that invalidated the promise and the fact that he had offered the buy-out.

"That should have made you happy. Isn't it what you wanted?" Karen asked when she had finished.

"Sure. I'm happy."

Karen laughed. "If that's your version of happiness, I'd hate to see depression."

"He gave me two choices. The other was to marry him."

"Oh." Karen put three spoonfuls of sugar in her tea and stirred it thoroughly before saying anything else. "I don't suppose that sat too well with you."

"I don't suppose so," Molly repeated grimly.

"You feel pretty miserable, huh?"

"That's an understatement," Molly said with a sad laugh.

Karen went on. "You're kind of sick to your stomach. You ache all over on the inside, like a horse kicked you. You lose track of time. You wonder how you're going to have energy to get up the stairs to bed, let alone get out of it tomorrow. You feel hopeless and empty and more rotten than you ever have in your life."

Molly smiled. "Those are my symptoms all right, Doc."

"That's how I felt. But you think you'd feel worse than this if you gave marriage to Ben a chance?"

Molly rolled her eyes. "Sneaky. Very sneaky."

"You know, if you don't risk failure, you don't have any chance at all of success."

Molly didn't say anything for a moment. She sipped her tea, wiped the ring the glass had made on the table and set it back down. Then she shook her head. "I just don't believe a woman can trust a man. I can't help looking at his family, even at his parents after forty-some years of marriage and thinking that at any time those same men could change their minds and take off."

Karen tasted her tea and put another spoonful of sugar in it. "I know I'm the last person to argue the other side of this, but since I'm the only one around, here goes. After Dave called off your wedding, you seemed to think every man was just like Dad, that not one of them could make a commitment and stick to it. You seemed to decide that from then on you were going to avoid them all. I'm sorry, Molly, but I think that's overreacting. It may have made you safe from what Mama went through, from what I'm going through now, but that isolation has left you incapable of spotting a trustworthy man when you find one."

"Meaning Ben is different from our father, from Carl?" Molly contributed dubiously.

Karen shrugged. "Like I said, I'm not a good judge. But I think if you look at him objectively, there's a lot in his favor."

"We haven't known him long enough or well enough to say that."

"You're just being contrary." Karen shooed away Molly's skepticism and laid her opinion out, anyway. "A promise is a commitment, isn't it? And until today when he realized he sort of got tricked into it, he was willing to go to some pretty far lengths to keep that promise. It would have been easier not to, and I'm sure it would be to his advantage to own everything by himself. But still, he stuck to it. He's been in the same business, the same location for nearly ten years. And remember I worked with him—his employees all respect and like him, and they know they can go to him with any problem they have. He even baby-sits for old girlfriends—now that's loyalty."

"Mmm," Molly mused wryly. "And dashes off to help deliver their babies."

"Because he's responsible, reliable and caring," Karen went on without missing a beat. "He puts other people before himself, and that's not something that could ever be said of our father. I hate to admit it, but it's not something that can be said of Carl. What that tells me is that you can believe he'll be that way in a relationship with you, too. And that's not something to throw away out of fear of anything."

Molly's mind was so full of turmoil that she barely noticed when Karen stood up and pulled her purse back onto her shoulder. "And I really hate iced tea," her sister said finally, taking her glass to the sink.

"I just don't know if I could take it if it didn't succeed," Molly thought out loud, staring into her own glass.

"You might never have to," Karen pointed out, picking up the box of toys and stray socks Molly had gathered up for her and left in a corner of the kitchen. Then she went to Molly, squeezed her shoulder and said in a voice choked with tears, "And if you do, you'll survive that, too." Then Karen bent over, gave her a little hug and left.

Molly stayed at the kitchen table, barely aware that her sister had gone. There was too much validity in what Karen had said about the kind of man Ben was. In fact, she couldn't think of anything at all that made him seem like her father.

She loved him. Maybe if she had never met him, never felt the way he made her feel, she could have continued living in her cocoon of distrust.

Molly suddenly knew that it was time to believe in a promise again. To believe in Ben.

Chapter Twelve

The best laid plans...

Molly didn't have the slightest idea what hospital Paula Brazos was in. It took her until midnight, making phone calls to every hospital in the phone book, to find out the woman had been admitted to Rose Medical Center. Once she knew that, all she could do was pace like an expectant father and call every hour on the hour. Her plan was to go to Ben's apartment the minute she found out that the baby had been delivered and ambush him as he came home.

Finally when she called the hospital at four she was informed that Paula Brazos had been taken to the delivery room.

Any time now...

Molly put on her slacks and slipped a silk blouse over her head. No bra. It felt cool and exciting:

Her eyes burned something fierce. She hadn't slept more than four hours a night in the last week, even with Nancy's chamomile tea. Not sleeping at all tonight on top of that was bound to leave her eyes bloodshot. Not too alluring. So once she was dressed she scooted back on her bed and pulled the phone into her lap. Carefully resting her head back against the pillow, she closed her eyes. Just for a minute. Just until four forty-five when she'd call again....

Everything would be all right. He loved her. He had said so even earlier tonight when she was turning down his proposal. She'd have Ben and a houseful of kids, just as the Boyds did. Christmas and holidays and summer picnics. Birthdays and anniversaries...lots of anniversaries...

The next thing Molly knew she had a cramp in her neck and she was in an uncomfortable slump. She tried to stretch her head back and hit the wall.

Then she remembered.

She opened her eyes with a jolt. There was bright sunshine seeping through a crack between the bottom of the shade and the window. What time was it? She blinked the sleep from her eyes and tried to focus on her clock radio on the nightstand.

Eleven-ten. It registered like a bolt of lightning.

She swung her legs off the bed and caught sight of herself in the mirror. So much for being irresistible. Her hair was flat on one side, her silk blouse was wrinkled, her slacks were as creased as if she had spent hours sitting on a plane.

"Just take it easy and slow down, Molly," she told herself, trying to think of a new plan.

Where would Ben be? Home. If the baby still hadn't been born at nearly five this morning, he probably would have gone home to get some sleep.

She ran a quick brush through her hair and slapped at the wrinkles in her clothes as she charged down the stairs and out to her car. Damn, damn, damn, why had she fallen asleep? She didn't want Ben to have any more time than he already had to think about what she had said and done, to get mad . . . or madder, to decide he really didn't love her and he was better off without someone so distrustful.

Ben's vintage Jaguar was not in the parking lot outside his apartment, so Molly made a U-turn and headed for Boyd's. She drove too fast and then, distracted by her thoughts, missed the turn into the office park and had to make another U-turn—this one illegal—to get back.

But once she had wound through the lot that accommodated four restaurants and three office towers, she spotted the black Jaguar. Breathing a sigh of relief, she pulled into the nearest parking space and bounded out of her car.

Then she had second thoughts.

What if she had just gone too far? Worse yet, what if he really was like her father and as soon as the pursuit was over and she accepted his proposal, he bolted?

Maybe she was better off alone, after all.

No, no, no! She didn't want to end up like her father. Ben wasn't like him, and *she* wouldn't be like him, either.

Molly took a breath and went into Boyd's. It was cool and dark and quiet. The lunch rush hadn't begun, and only two tables had customers at them. The hostess smiled at her.

"One for lunch?" she asked.

"No," Molly said in a rush. She suddenly realized no one there knew her. "I need to see Ben, please. I'm...a friend."

"I'm sorry, but he isn't here," the young, well-dressed woman said very formally.

"He has to be here," Molly blurted out, and then tried to sound more normal. "I saw his car in the parking lot."

"He was here, but he left over an hour ago for an appointment with his brother," the hostess said suspiciously.

"With his brother, Rick?"

The young woman eyed her. "Yes. Do you know Rick?"

Molly's frustration level was high. "Yes, I know Rick," she snapped. "Where did they meet? At Marie Callendar's?"

The hostess frowned. "No. I believe Ben was going to Rick's office. Would you care to take a table and wait?"

"Where is Rick's office?"

The young woman glanced around her as if she needed help.

Molly tried to sound more reasonable. "I'm Molly Mercer, Ben's partner, and it's very important that I find him. It's an emergency."

"Molly Mercer," the young woman repeated as if she vaguely knew the name. "Oh, you must be Karen's sister. Well, I guess if it's an emergency. Do you see that high-rise office building at the far end of the parking lot?" She pointed out the door in the direction of a black glass structure. "I think Rick's office is there."

Molly could have kissed her. Instead she thanked her profusely and left the restaurant in such a hurry that she nearly knocked over a group of elderly women on their way in.

She dodged cars coming and going, finally arriving at the lobby of the building the hostess had pointed to.

Richard A. Boyd, Attorney-at-law, it said on the directory, Suite 405. Molly pushed the elevator button and waited. She tapped her foot nervously, slid her hands into her pockets and then back out again, adjusted her purse onto her left shoulder and then changed it to her right.

Finally the elevator doors opened on the fourth floor. Molly stepped out, then spun around to find that Rick's office was directly in front of the elevator. Ben would be there, and she could apologize and all the havoc her stupidity had wreaked would be over. She hoped.

An older woman sat behind the desk in the reception area. Looking up at Molly as she entered, the secretary smiled. "May I help you?"

"I need to see Ben Boyd," she informed her a little breathlessly.

"*Ben* Boyd?" the woman repeated dimly. "I'm afraid you have the wrong office. This is *Richard* Boyd's practice."

Molly forced herself to be patient. "I know that. But Ben is his brother and he's meeting with *Richard* Boyd now."

"I'm sorry, I'm sitting in for the regular secretary today, and all I know is that Mr. *Richard* Boyd is in conference right now and can't be disturbed."

Molly snapped. "He's in conference with his brother, *Ben* Boyd. And I have to see Ben Boyd right now. It's an emergency."

But what had worked on the hostess had no effect on this woman. She merely repeated that she couldn't disturb the conference.

Molly's heart was pounding, her palms were damp, her head was light. She knew Ben was behind that door, and nothing was going to stop her from seeing him before it was too late. She stepped around the desk and, ignoring the secretary's shock and outrage, she burst through the door.

Up came three faces, one of them Rick's—quite perturbed, one of them a very solemn man and the other a teary-eyed woman.

But no Ben.

Molly wanted to sink through the floor. "I . . . I'm sorry," she stammered. "I thought Ben was in here." She had never been more embarrassed in her life. As she closed the door, she heard Rick call her name, but she closed it, anyway.

A second later he was in the reception area, smiling with his mouth and frowning with his brow. "Molly, wait a minute." He stopped her retreat with a hand on her arm.

Molly swallowed and felt heat suffuse her face. She couldn't speak.

"Ben was here," Rick told her kindly, "but he went across to the bank to arrange for a loan...." His voice drifted off as if he had said something he shouldn't have.

Molly felt sick to her stomach. She was too late, she thought. He was finished with her.

"Molly? Are you all right?" Rick said when she didn't answer, his hand still on her arm.

"I guess that's it," she said to herself.

Rick laughed sympathetically. "Don't be so fatalistic. You can still catch him," he suggested. "The bank is in the building right next door."

Maybe this fiasco of a morning was an omen. Maybe she should quit fighting fate and give in.

But she loved him. She had to tell him that. She had to see if she could salvage what was between them.

She swallowed again. "I'm sorry for..." She nodded toward the inner-office door, too chagrined even to put it into words.

"It's okay. We're just hashing out a prenuptial agreement. I'll tell them you're chasing my brother to accept his marriage proposal and it'll break some of the tension. That is what you're doing, isn't it?"

"If he'll have me," she whispered.

"Right next door," he repeated. "Go for it." And he gave Molly a little push.

She realized she had forgotten to even say goodbye only when she was two floors down in the elevator. Again she rushed out into the parking lot, dodging cars on her way to the next building. It was also glass, the interior of the bank visible from the outside.

And there was Ben, sitting at a desk under a sign that read New Loans.

Without taking her eyes off him, Molly took a moment to smooth her hair. Even from a distance he looked resigned and...

She moved considerably slower as she went into the bank. Dragging her feet was what she was doing. There was something so forbidding about his expression. So determined. So closed and final.

But then how else would he look? She had left him believing there was no chance of a future for them.

At least she hoped that was the reason, and not that he had made the same decision himself.

"Hi," she said, grimacing slightly at the inanity of it as she came up behind him, yet not knowing what else to say.

She only sensed that the man behind the desk looked up at her when Ben did because her gaze never left Ben. He frowned at her, and she saw how tired he looked beneath his clean, impeccably neat appearance. He didn't answer her greeting. Instead he cocked one of those slightly bushy eyebrows at her.

Molly's knees felt weak. She sat sideways in the empty chair beside him. "I need to talk to you," she said.

"Do you?" he asked snidely.

"Please," she said under her breath.

"I'm busy at the moment getting you what you want," he said with a note of challenge in his voice.

"I'd rather talk to you first."

"It seems to me that everything's been said."

"Well, maybe there's been a new development."

Ben laughed ironically. "That would be news since I'm beginning to doubt that you're capable of developing past the twelve-year-old kid who got left behind."

Molly couldn't speak. She just stared at him, her eyes locked with his.

"I'm sorry," he said with a sigh, shaking his head ruefully. "That was a low blow. I haven't had any sleep and I'm afraid I'm just not up to any more of the strategies of the Mercer-Northrup war." Then he faced the loan officer again. "Where do I sign?"

Molly didn't want him to sign anything. Somehow it made everything seem too final. She still wanted the buy-out, but not before fixing things between them, not before discussing it all more rationally, not before making sure he knew she wanted him, too.

Molly panicked and turned to the bank official herself. "You don't want to loan this man money. He's a bad risk," she blurted out. Then, in a theatrical gesture she reached across the desk, snatched up the papers in front of the man and in one rapid motion, tore them in half.

Ben shook his head slowly and held up several papers that were on the desk in front of him. "These are mine, Molly."

"And now Mr. and Mrs. Leland will have to make another trip in to redo theirs," the banker put in very dryly, his disgust echoing in his voice.

For the second time in half an hour Molly wanted to sink through the floor. Or maybe just vaporize and waft away. Today was turning into a comedy of errors she didn't think was very funny. But the only thing she could do now was tough it through. Her whole life was at stake.

"I'm sorry, but if you only knew what a bad risk this man is, you'd thank me."

That brought another breathy, bitter laugh from Ben. "That certainly sums up your opinion of me."

Molly turned to see him looking at her again, his eyes unreadable. "Just for some things. Not for others."

"For instance?" Ben asked conversationally.

She met his gaze squarely, searching for any sign of encouragement. The hint of a sparkle gave her the courage to answer him. "Marriage," she said softly.

"I think you're a fair marriage risk. And as a business partner...I understand there's no one more trustworthy or reliable."

"I'm trustworthy and reliable as a marriage partner, too," he added defensively. Then he leaned across the arm of his chair until his nose was nearly pressed to hers and slowly enunciated every word he said to her. "And I keep my promises. Every damned one of them. Right up to the end."

He picked up the loan papers in front of him and held them up to her. "Do you know what this is?" he asked curtly. "It's a loan to give you the money you would have made from my buying you out. But it is not a buy-out."

Molly was confused. "It isn't?"

"No, it isn't. I don't know what part it played in your head, but I know what going back on my word did in mine. I couldn't live with myself. It doesn't matter what your father's motives were. It doesn't matter what kind of rotten things he did in his life. It only mattered to me that I had promised him I'd make sure you and Karen had a steady income from your shares of my restaurants. It matters more now, for my own reasons, that you still have that steady income. So, dammit, whether you like it or not, you're still a partner. You can consider this loan an investment in Mercer Moving and Storage, an investment in you that has nothing at all to do with John Northrup."

Molly sat back in her chair, stunned. "You would do that for me?"

"Of course I'd do it for you. Or at least I would have done it for you before you came in here to tear up other people's papers and tell this poor man I'm a lousy risk."

"Even after everything I said?" she mused, ignoring his last comments.

Ben shook his head. "It isn't altruistic. I figured this way we'd be double partners and we'd have to keep in contact. Eventually I thought I might convince you that I'm not the man your father was. That you could trust me."

Molly didn't know what to say. Her heart was in her throat. "You really are a nice man," she managed finally, a bare whisper as if she had just truly realized it.

Ben signed the papers and handed them to the banker who watched as if they had both lost their minds. "I'd appreciate it if you'd ignore her claim and process these. I'm sure you'll find my credit satisfactory." Then he took Molly's hand and led her out of the bank.

He didn't say a word as they crossed the two parking lots, went into Boyd's Restaurant, through the kitchen and into his office. Only when the door was closed and locked behind them did he face her, grasping both of her shoulders in his hands. "I love you, Molly. I'll do anything it takes to convince you that that won't change."

She smiled slowly, realizing only in that moment that she really did believe him. "I know. And I love you, too." Then she remembered the trust he was putting in her by borrowing the money to keep her business afloat. "I really think I can make Mercer Moving and Storage work if I can just get us out of this hole. It's like..." She fumbled for an explanation. "You don't carry car insurance because you're sure you're going to have an accident. You carry it just in case you do. My business is the same thing for me."

He was smiling softly at her. "It's okay. Because I know you're never going to have to file a claim. But if it makes you feel more secure, I'm all for it. It's your security and happiness that are the most important to me."

She believed that, too, and it was just another thing about Ben that set him apart from her father.

He pulled her into his arms. His mouth came down over hers, at first tenderly, renewing their bond, and then more intensely, hungrily. His lips parted, and his tongue found hers as his hands slid underneath her silk blouse. Finding her braless, he moaned deep in his throat.

"Did you come prepared to seduce me?" he asked hopefully.

Molly answered him only with a raised eyebrow and a mysterious smile. "I called the hospital all night long. I meant to be waiting at your apartment when you got home, but I fell asleep. What kind of baby did your friend have?"

"Another girl."

"Did you sleep at all?"

"I tried, but there was no way. So I decided to shower and put the wheels into motion for your money. My plan was to be waiting at *your* house when you got home tonight. But I was going to wear underwear." He kissed her again, and this time it was long and slow and deeply sensual.

"I want you . . . but not here," he said against her skin, his voice husky. "Too many interruptions and too little time and space. What do you say we both take the day off? I think we've earned it."

Molly could only moan her agreement. He drew his hands from her back around to her breasts, kneading them only a moment before he deserted her, pulling her blouse back into place.

"My apartment is messier than your house, but it's closer."

Then he took her hand, and together they snuck out the delivery door.

They reached his apartment in ten minutes flat. And then he nearly dragged her up the stairs.

Molly only noticed peripherally that his apartment was strewn with debris as he progressively undressed her on their way to the bedroom, adding her clothes to the clutter. But his bed was made, and the incongruity of that made her laugh.

"I can't stand to get into an unmade bed," he explained as he shed his own clothes and pressed her into the thick down quilt that covered it like a cream-colored cloud.

Lean and muscular, he snaked his way up until the length of his naked flesh met hers. His mouth came down on hers, and she welcomed the onslaught of his tongue. Then they came together, quickly, intensely, as if they had been without one another for months and months.

And when they had each climaxed in an explosion of joy, Ben rolled them so that, still joined, she was lying on top of him.

With her ear pressed to his chest, Molly could hear his heartbeat, strong and steady, his breath returning to normal.

"Will you marry me, Molly Mercer?" he asked in a passionate voice.

"Yes," she agreed with a little laugh.

"And then I'll spend the rest of my life proving to you that my vows are never broken, my commitments are for keeps and my promises are always kept,'' he said as formally as if they were standing at an altar right then.

"It's a deal," she agreed.

Ben tilted her face up to his and kissed her again, sweetly. And in the comfort of his arms, Molly knew that here was finally someone to turn to in times of good and bad, someone to share her joys and her burdens with, someone to walk with her through the rough times as well as the easy ones, someone for her to turn to. She wasn't alone to face everything on her own any more.

She really had found shelter from the storm. And a promise that would be kept.

*   *   *   *   *

Silhouette Special Edition

COMING NEXT MONTH

A QUESTION OF HONOR
Lindsay McKenna

When narcotics agent Kit Anderson went undercover, she landed up 'under the covers' with Coast Guard skipper Noah Trayhern! Fireworks explode in Lindsay McKenna's new series celebrating America's men (and women!) in uniform.

FOR ALL MY TOMORROWS
Debbie Macomber

Suddenly widowed Lynn Danfort had felt doubly bereft when her husband's best friend abruptly left town. Now, three years later, husky Ryder Matthews was back and he seemed to be offering far more than friendship.

KING OF HEARTS
Tracy Sinclair

When schoolteacher Stephanie Blair met dashing, evasive Morgan Destine, she didn't notice that the suave, mysterious stranger asked more questions than he answered. Who was he?

Silhouette Special Edition

COMING NEXT MONTH

FACE VALUE
Celeste Hamilton

Beau Collins was frantic — where would he find a
fresh face to launch a national ad, campaign? Then
he noticed the woman who lived next-door, quiet,
bespectacled Caitlin Welch...

HEATHER ON THE HILL
Barbara Faith

When outgoing American Blythe Warner and
Cameron McCabe impulsively got married the real
world came crashing in on them, spoiling their
enchantment. A Scottish earl and an unwed mother,
their lives were oceans apart.

REPEAT PERFORMANCE
Lynda Trent

Years ago, Jordan Landry had broken their
engagement — and Carley Kingston's heart — to
marry another woman. Now Jordan was back,
demanding a repeat performance! It would be silly
of Carley to trust him again, wouldn't it?

VOWS *LaVyrle Spencer* £2.99

When high-spirited Emily meets her father's new business rival, Tom, sparks fly, and create a blend of pride and passion in this compelling and memorable novel.

LOTUS MOON *Janice Kaiser* £2.99

This novel vividly captures the futility of the Vietnam War and the legacy it left. Haunting memories of the beautiful Lotus Moon fuel Buck Michael's dangerous obsession, which only Amanda Parr can help overcome.

SECOND TIME LUCKY *Eleanor Woods* £2.75

Danielle has been married twice. Now, as a young, beautiful widow, can she back-track to the first husband whose life she left in ruins with her eternal quest for entertainment and the high life?

These three new titles will be out in bookshops from September 1989.

W🌑RLDWIDE

Available from Boots, Martins, John Menzies, W.H. Smith, Woolworths and other paperback stockists.